The
Planting
Rite

Book One of The Rememberer's Tales

The Planting Rite: Book One of the Rememberer's Tales
Second Edition by C. L. Parker
Copyright © 2006 C. L. Parker
All rights reserved.

Edited by Daña Alder. Certain book design by Eva Bee.
Cover design and Illustration by Anne Marie Forrester.
Images provided by Dreamstime.com
Copyright © 2006 *Creatrix Vision Spun Fiction LLC*. All rights reserved.

ISBN–10: 0–9760604–3–4
ISBN–13: 978–0–9760604–3–7

Published by *Creatrix Vision Spun Fiction LLC*,
A *Creatrix Books LLC* company

P.O. Box 366
Cottage Grove, WI 53527

Printed in the USA

Acknowledgements

I would like to acknowledge all the wonderful women of the
Re–formed Congregation of the Goddess, International
for their support and inspiration.
She lives!

And to Lauren Heller for helping plant the seeds
so many years ago.
You will always be my Sarano.

"If you remember a time when women were free and our culture reflected that freedom in every action and concept this book will not surprise you.
Parker explores this time and weaves a tale that celebrates what women's culture was and can be."

This book is dedicated to Deb, Chelsea, Holly and Kyle.
You make my life joyful and meaningful every day.

THE PLANTING RITE

Book One of the Rememberer's Tales

Kip Parker

Creatrix Vision Spun Fiction LLC,
A *Creatrix Books LLC* company

Summer, 1984 C.E.
Kip

The threadbare, lavender bandana was already limp with warm sweat as I mopped the back of my neck. My leg muscles throbbed with fatigue. After hiking for hours through rolling hills covered in pine forest, I heard no sound except the insistent crunching of my boots on the thick underlayment of dried needles and ferns. I could not tell where the road was anymore. Raw blisters hurt my feet, even in the soft leather of my Doc Martens, and I had run out of trail mix that morning. Thankfully, the air was beginning to cool now that the sun had set. I approached a light that I could see through the trees, hoping that I might find a kind local resident who could tell me how to get back to town.

As I reached the clearing, I saw a dilapidated house through the twilight. The wood was weathered and unpainted, darkened by time and recent rain. Still, a merry glow flickered from the windows and spoke of warmth. Smells of coffee and something sweetly spiced reached out to me, and my stomach rumbled loudly. I could see into the rear windows from my vantage point but saw no one moving inside. I decided to go around to the front, where an approaching stranger might seem less startling to any occupants.

The weathered boards that passed for a porch stood less than a foot off the ground, supported by cement blocks. Two crooked rocking chairs sat precariously with a small wooden table between them. On the table was a large earthen bowl that held only a gnarled old paring knife. The vivid blue of the bowl stood out from the dull colors of the porch and cottage.

As I rounded the corner, my eyes were drawn to a spot in the yard where a bonfire licked the black sky. That's where I saw her.

She looked as if she sat waiting, her ancient face in shadow. The hairs on the back of my neck prickled. She sat on a ragged stump, adding sticks to the ravenous inferno before her. With each bite, the flames surged and threw sparks into the night like confetti from a Pride Parade float full of drag queens. She looked up slowly, her beady, black eyes glittering like polished obsidian.

"Kip," she said.

I was stunned that she knew my name, but the cynic in me thought, "I've seen this act before, usually inside a dark tent at a carnival or on a crowded street in Soho." She looked like every other so–called Gypsy tarot reader I had ever encountered. Her plain black dress and garish shawl even reminded me of Hecate on a card in my own deck.

I had just about decided that the wily woman saw me as another easy target, as she looked ready to make a sale. Her black eyes glinted at me, the penetrating gaze scanning me up and down. I expected her to say she could teach me all the mysteries and then name her price, but she never did. She simply raised her hand and beckoned me nearer.

As I made my way toward her, my boots sank into soft earth and I looked down. I had almost stepped onto a tilled patch of soft loam. "Not smart, Kip," I scolded myself. The last thing I wanted to do was make the resident angry by walking through her garden. I stepped around the patch and moved into the circle of firelight.

"Finally, you have come. It was almost too late. I am the last."

"The last what?" I blurted.

She looked at me as if I were a slow child, her face revealing a balance of pity and annoyance. Over the following months, she would look at me many times that very same way.

I was tramping around Europe on a wild chase to find a map to my spiritual beliefs. In the anonymous self–help program I had joined, I heard lots of advice about how I had to find a "higher power," but I could not and do not accept their version of a bearded, ancient white man as creator and judge.

They told me there was no cost for their help in regaining my life from the abyss of addiction, but in the end, their actions demanded that I succumb to their view of the universe. They said if I searched hard enough, I would find a spiritual path acceptable to both them and me. Well, they were half right.

And so it began. I read books about many religions; I attended different gatherings and services. Some of the congregations I visited during those days claimed to welcome everyone. In most cases "everyone" didn't include lesbian leather–clad, recovering addicts. Even when I was welcomed, it was as an outsider. I felt like the weird spinster aunt at Thanksgiving dinner: welcomed but scrutinized.

I knew there was more. I knew that somewhere there was a place I could feel like I belonged. So far, my religious experiences included the fiery judgmental god of American fundamentalist Christians, the kindly father–figure of European Christianity, and at last the fussy, politically correct representations of female deities the witches to whom I turned for guidance had shown me. Maybe the problem wasn't where I was looking. Maybe I just wasn't ready to be still long enough to hear my own heart.

In any case, I took off in search of something more, something bigger, something older, something that looked more like me. I don't know which I had less of, money or sense; it was a close call. But here I was, somewhere in the dark woods of Eastern Europe, searching for a mirror for my soul.

I almost walked away that first night. The city–bred fear of strangers almost won out over the quiet little voice inside that urged me to stay and listen. Why I lingered, I can't say, but I did. I listened to her, helped her fix the hole in the porch, and learned to live with the seasons.

Her name was Aranna, and she shared with me stories about her Tribe through many generations. The first ancestors she spoke of lived in a village in what is now Romania. They settled long ago on a plateau between the Olt River and the Transylvanian Alps only a few miles from where we sat, she said.

I asked what made them choose that particular place. She said that before they settled and built the village, they wandered, following the seasons and gathering food wherever they found it. The leader at that time discovered that they could make plants grow where they wanted them to, and she picked a site for their village with everything they needed: water, trees, and rich, level ground to till.

Was this woman really telling me that her ancestors invented horticulture? I thought it was preposterous at first, but there was something in the authority with which she spoke that kept my mind open.

Her words are with me to this day, drifting into my dreams and often running in the back of my mind as audio wallpaper. "Things have not always been as they are now. Nothing is as it seems. The world is much older than most people think. And The Mother has been with us always. But to see Her, you must have the eyes."

I spent what seemed like years listening to the many stories she had saved. She claimed to be The Rememberer, one of the

"Hesh–taz," and the last of her Tribe. I asked if that meant she was a follower of Hestia. She laughed, saying that, on the contrary, Hestia was a descendant who was named for the Hesh–taz, a group that apparently was several thousand years older than the Goddess we know today. She thought it hilarious that young women revered the one named Hestia.

"Some day," she chuckled, "I will tell you stories about that girl! She was a wild one, full of piss and vinegar. Never once did the flame go out while she was hearth–keeper, but it was not because of her vigilance. No, she was always out of the village, running here and there and getting into trouble. Some said her red hair was what made her wild. Some said she got animals to help her guard the flame. I don't know. But I do know she was nothing like the legend later invented by the Romans."

She assured me that when I met another descendant of the Tribe, I would know instantly. She said I would feel as if I knew everything about her before she spoke one word to me. In years since, that has happened several times, and other women have told me of that same sense of bonding.

For years after I returned to New York, I said nothing about my time with her, not to lovers, sponsors, or friends, convinced they would not believe me. Even after I began to explore Dianic Wicca, I spoke of her only to a trusted few, and when I did talk of her Tribe, I disguised what I knew as something I had imagined. I even wrote a play about her that was performed at the Women's Alternative Community Center on Long Island, thanks to the encouragement of my Tribe sisters there.

Much later, after years of self–help groups, therapy, geographic cures, and countless relationships, I found myself in Indiana, working in an office and helping raise my first child, Chelsea. She was and is the light of my days, but as wonderful an experience as parenting is, there came a day when I realized that I still searched for a place where I belonged.

One day I stumbled into the office of the Re–Formed

Congregation of the Goddess, International (RCGI) in Madison, Wisconsin. I looked into the eyes of Jade River and knew I had found the descendant of the Hearth Queen. Over time, I revealed to Jade many of the tales I had heard in Europe, and I was never surprised that she already seemed to know them. I always considered myself a writer but had never succeeded in getting any work published. Jade suggested I think about self–publishing or print–on–demand.

As happens when one invites change, change came, but not as I envisioned. One day I walked into work and was given the news that I was being "downsized," along with my 10–person staff and 120 hourly employees. The company offered me a generous severance package and a pat on the back.

Suddenly I had all the time in the world. I filed for unemployment and began to write this book, sending pages to Jade and other friends as I finished them, to test the believability of the tale.

Still, two more years went by before I said to Jade, "It's time to submit it to a printer." I sent the completed galleys to Patricia Monaghan, who was gracious and kind to a newly hatched author. She wrote some thoughts for the cover, as did Jade.

In this first book I relate some of the tales told by my ancestor, The Rememberer, around her fire in the woods. I chose to tell first the stories from the first year of the settlement. There have been many books written about the end of the matriarchy, and I know and will write those stories, too. But I needed this first book to be about the time before the change, the time when we were still free.

The two– or three thousand years of "history" taught in most cultures is a mere drop in the bucket of Time. For untold generations before horse riders of the steppes forced their male–dominated worldview onto all they encountered, there was a simpler way of life, a way that somewhere in our deepest knowing, we remember and still long for.

In modern times it has been hard for me to grasp how women lived before the influence of patriarchy. I have spent my entire life fighting the ghosts, triggers, and emotional wounds of this male–dominated world. I tried to comprehend an entire lifetime without this struggle, and it seemed to be the utopia of which we had all dreamed. I asked myself if deep down in an untapped river of memory, I did remember after all. During my time in the forest, she told me that we all do remember. All who are descendants of the Tribes remember. Today, I believe she was right.

The scholars and explorers of our time have found words, sculptures, and drawings on cave walls from the old times around the globe. I honor their work. I have read much of Gimbutas, Monaghan, Stone, and Walker. Their interpretations fed my soul during my darkest, loneliest days and inspired me to look deeper.

The Hearth and Hunt Queens of our time, Z. Budapest, Starhawk, Kim Duckett, Letecia Layson, and especially Jade River, have guided me and soothed my heart with their words and examples. By at last telling the stories behind the facts, by learning to trust the voice inside, I affirm and honor their work.

These stories are for anyone who has gazed on a picture of an ancient, painted vase and wondered, "Who was the woman who filled this with water? How did she live with her sisters?" These are the stories that I write, ones to awaken memories in descendants of the Tribe. I am a lucky woman. After half–a–lifetime of searching, I have found my place in the world.

Of course, I cannot tell all the things I learned from The Rememberer; some were for certain ears only. The old woman not only trusted my memory, but also my vision and judgment as well. A true bard does not tell all her tales — she knows when to honor the silence, and I do. I remember and pass on what needs to be passed on, as she taught me.

It has been many years since I last saw her. I am sure she has walked through the gates of Hecate by now. I hope I make her proud.

But I have said enough about me. These books are not intended to be the story of a writer, they are the stories of a race, my race, maybe yours, too. While today only fragments of pottery and fat little female statues remain for our scholars to piece together, fragments of memories can flirt with us in the dark at the Michigan night stage — memories that make us all want to stand together and howl when the moon is round on rocky hills in Ireland, or Germany, or anywhere; memories that make the woman we have just met seem so familiar; memories that make us create theories about who and what we are channeling. Racial memory . . . ? Maybe. Maybe one day with a few helpful hints, we will all remember. May the Great Bear Mother grant it.

Many blessings,
Kip Parker

Spring
3783 B.C.E.

"Jori! Do not run there! Mother will be angry!" Kelan's strident warning came to Jori across the sunlit meadow.

Jori felt the squish of soft black dirt as it slid between her toes and swallowed most of her foot. Realizing she was walking on newly turned earth, she gingerly stepped away, shaking her foot to dislodge the warm chunks. She remembered when she stepped in a pile of dung as a child on the trail, and this felt just like that.

She sighed heavily and shrugged at her sister as she viewed Mama's garden. No matter how many times her mother explained it, Jori still could not believe that plants for food were going to pop up from this patch of ground some day.

"I still do not know what all the fuss is," she said out loud, folding her arms across her chest.

"Do not worry, Jori. I am having trouble getting used to the idea, too," said her friend Ara, mimicking Jori's stance. "But your mother said not to step in her 'gar–den.'" The unfamiliar word fell clumsily from her tongue.

Jori backed away from the tilled area's boundary. With a huff, she flopped in the tall grass, squinting back at the garden. She had never seen anything like it before. How could anyone predict where a certain plant would grow? Her mother's magic was powerful, maybe the most powerful in the Tribe. She was Hearth Queen after all, so Jori was accustomed to seeing magic in her daily life. But she wondered whether even her powerful mother could command Nature, and so she asked.

Jori remembered how Mama's blue eyes sparkled and her thick, reddish mane cascaded as she threw back her head in laughter. She told Jori that the trick to any good magic was to understand and work WITH the flow of Nature, not try to command Her.

Garnet explained that she and Devin spent many seasons watching how plants grew in the wild. She simply took what she learned from The Mother and applied it to her observations of plants, believing the plants might follow their nature in a place that was convenient for the Tribe. Plants did not know why they grew where they grew. If they had enough land, sun, and water, seeds would grow into plants, and these plants could feed the Tribe. Mama had chosen an area for the garden that had rich black soil, plenty of sun, and water close by, and she asked the Hunters to prepare the ground.

The Tribe's Hunters seemed eager to do Garnet's bidding, no matter what the request. Perhaps, Jori thought, Mama spent time studying them, too, for when Mama asked, the Hunters worked for three solid days with tools of wood and stone to turn the large patch of earth she selected into long, straight rows. Some grumbled about wasted effort, but still they performed the tasks.

Jori remembered how the freshly turned black earth smelled and how the exposed, fat worms squirmed quickly back into the soil, as if the sunlight hurt them. Jori enjoyed her assignment of carrying water skins to the workers. She liked the sturdy Hunters and was happy for any task that took her into their midst. Now, when she stood at the end of a row, the lines that the Hunters had formed in the earth looked like little braids worn by women of other tribes.

Once the rows were prepared, Garnet walked alongside them and poked little seeds from last year's found plants into the dirt, spacing them a small distance apart. Jori had never seen plants grow in long lines before, and she asked Mama what part of Nature she had studied to learn about something that never was. Her question made Devin and the Hunters laugh out loud; sometimes Jori did not understand grown women's jokes at all.

Thinking about it all over again, Jori had even more questions: How did Mama plan to keep out goats and rabbits? Would they not just eat anything that popped out of the ground? What about birds? She sighed from the weight of all these concerns.

Kelan's shadow fell over Jori and she looked up to see her sister scowling, hands on her hips. Ara fell to the grass next to Jori and looked defiant.

Kelan and the other children had been chasing butterflies in a meadow near the village. Tall, flaxen flowers had just begun blooming, and the meadow grass was almost high enough to hide the girls as they crouched and watched the colorful creatures flit around in living clouds.

"Come on! Come and play with us!" Kelan demanded, her dark hair hanging in wild tangles. She impatiently brushed it away from her face.

"I am tired of chasing butterflies. There are too many. I would rather just watch them." Jori waved her arm across the field.

"How about we take a walk by the river," Ara suggested.

"We are not supposed to go there without an adult, Ara. You know that!" another girl whined.

The others gathered around Kelan's flanks. They always seemed to stand like that, Jori noticed, all in a gaggle with

Kelan at the front. Kelan and her row of ducklings, Jori thought. Disgusting!

"Come on," cajoled Jori, trying to persuade her sister and ignoring the ducklings, "we have to have some fun this summer before our lessons start."

"That does not mean we should do things that are forbidden, Jori," one girl insisted, crossing her arms over her chest. "You break the rules if you want. We will not, and when we tell your mothers, you will be punished."

Jori suddenly stood and leaned forward until her nose almost touched that of the little tattletale. She turned her head, slowly scanning the entire group, her ice–blue eyes locking with each duckling in turn. Each one looked away nervously. "Go to my mother if you wish," she said in a quiet, slow voice, "but I will remember if you do . . . and this campsite has plenty of snakes!" Jori spit on the ground and walked away quickly toward the village, Ara at her side.

Whispering excitedly, "What snakes are you . . ." Ara began.

"Shhh! Last summer that one tattled to my mother one afternoon. Later that night she found a snake in her sleeping furs, and she assumed I put it there."

"DID YOU??" Ara was awed by the apparent ruthlessness.

Jori grinned. "Of course not," she said implacably, "but our lessons teach us to let others believe what they will, right?"

Ara laughed with glee. Suddenly her grin faded and she stopped in her tracks. "Lessons," her shoulders slumped dejectedly. "They start after the summer . . ."

"Sure," Jori kept her voice light and her tone cheerful despite the chill Ara's words sent up her spine, "but look at the bright side. You only have to endure lessons until Yule. The rest of us are old enough to begin our apprentice training this winter, and we will be in training forever! Come on, though, it is not even the equinox yet!" Jori leapt into a fast sprint toward the river, laughing. Ara hesitated, then ran to catch up.

Jori knew well what lay in store for them when the leaves turned. Many older children had come to Mama for lessons, and when she was small, she watched them sitting around Garnet in a circle and wanted to join in. But now she felt different. It was not the lessons that she dreaded, it was the coming Yule–time decision.

The first season's training was easy for the daughter of a leader, as the initial studies were general. Children learned about the Tribe's society, expected behavior, and the responsibilities of adults. They learned how events were planned and how the Tribe made decisions that affected everyone.

When winter came, both boy– and girl– children had to decide whether to stay with the women's Tribe or join the men's Tribe in the coming spring. Boy children always wanted to join the men, and girl children always wanted to stay with the women. Jori did not know if a boy had ever stayed or if a girl had ever gone, but it must be possible since every child was asked. It did not matter so much this year, as there were no boys at choosing age.

The choice of Tribe was not the choice she dreaded, anyway. She knew she always wanted to stay with the women, but children who stayed also had to tell the Council the kind of work they wanted to do as adults. Once a child stated her choice, all the adult women were invited to comment, then the Tribe as a whole either endorsed the idea or rejected it and named another line of work. Because of the high value the Tribe placed on individual choice, there had to be very compelling reasons to reject a child's desires, but it had happened in the past, however rarely.

This moment of choice was what Jori feared most, and her heart raced as she thought of it. She already knew her desire. There was only one path she could take and be true to her heart and her nature, but she doubted the Elders would ever approve.

If they rejected her choice, she could either accept their decision or rebel. She was not sure she had the strength to stand against all of them, but she decided not to let her dread spoil the few days left in her last free summer.

Jori wondered what her life would be like at the garden's next planting. Only the loyal Ara understood how important this coming spring was to her. Now that they walked alone near the water, Jori gave voice to her dreams.

"Ara, do you think I could ever be the Hunt Queen, like Devin? I love going on hunts and building things!" Jori tossed a rock into the water.

"You would be the best one ever!" Ara looked up at her admiringly. "But are you not expected to follow your mother's path?"

"I do not wish to BE Hearth Queen!" Jori said stubbornly. "I do not like naming babies or blessing houses or settling disputes!"

"Me, either," Ara agreed. "I want to build things, too!"

"Yes, and walk the woods at night and learn to shoot a bow!" Her feet stomped the grass as her gait became more determined. "They will not make me choose something I do not want!"

"Do not worry, Jori." Ara tossed another rock and watched it splash. "Something will happen, and it will be all right. It just has to be."

"What?" Jori stopped and looked at her little friend. "What will happen?"

Ara looked directly into Jori's eyes. "I do not know, but something will."

"HOW do you know?"

"Because I have never seen Nature force a Bear cub to become a fish, and that is the same thing as trying to make you the Hearth Queen. It would be bad for you AND bad for the Tribe, and The Mother will not allow it." Jori's stone skipped halfway across the river's surface, and she looked at the serene face of her little friend. Ara smiled reassuringly.

Jori suddenly smirked and nudged her friend playfully on the shoulder. "Want to go swimming?"

Ara's arms flailed wildly as she tried to keep her balance on the slope. She regained her feet, shoved Jori hard, and the girls laughed as they grappled for dominance. The mud on the bank crumbled, and they both slid into the water!

Jori fell with a splat onto her bottom. She heard Ara laughing behind and above her, apparently still standing. Jori would fix that!

"Want a hand up?" Ara asked innocently. The water was shallow, and Jori's hands sunk into muck as she pushed herself upright. She rose with a big glob of mud in her hand and threw it at her friend. Chaos ensued. Eventually, Ara signaled an end to the match, crying, "Enough, enough! I am drowning in muck!"

The girls rinsed themselves in the cold water, still laughing and splashing, and climbed the bank to a warm grassy patch where they lay together in silence.

Jori closed her eyes. The sun was warm and the grassy bank, soft. She thought again of the garden and the new way of life the Tribe pursued in this place.

So far as Jori knew, it all began several years ago when Mama and Devin first gathered seeds. They planted them in places that they marked specially and went back later to see if anything had happened. This was what her mother meant when she said they studied Nature.

During the past two winters, Garnet enlisted women of the Tribe to save seeds from harvested plants. These were carefully sorted and stored by the old ones of the village who also sang special chants over them. When this year's thaw came and the earth warmed, the Hearth Queen convinced the Tribe to lay plans for a permanent village.

The Hunt Queen and her helpers turned the ground, and the Hearth Queen herself carefully placed seeds into the rich earth, finishing with the last of the seeds just yesterday. Tonight, a ritual and feast were being held to celebrate. Garnet called it the Planting Rite, and even Jori had a role: When her mother gave a special signal, Jori would enter the ritual circle with a basket of seeds and Kelan would enter with a basket of pouches. That was all she knew; the rest of the ritual was, as always, secret.

If Mama's garden plan worked, the Tribe would live in this place both summer and winter instead of traveling with the seasons. Jori wondered if she would see more of her father if the men's Tribe always knew where to find them? That might be nice, she thought. For all of his strangeness, her father always treated her kindly.

Jori wondered if the men's Tribe might ever try staying in one place, perhaps gathering the great herds they followed and somehow getting them to stay as well. She laughed out loud. That was ridiculous! Sheep, elk, and cattle were not like kartof, to be kept wherever people wanted! She was not even sure that kartof and lentils would grow at her mother's command. They would all learn the answer together.

Jori's nose tickled. She shook her head to clear the feeling, but it persisted.

"Jori, wake up. We have to go home now," Ara whispered in her ear as she ran a blade of grass under her nose. Jori sat up groggily. "You fell asleep," Ara smiled. "We are all dried off, and we need to get back before one of those ducklings sends someone for us."

At the fire circle, the Fire Keepers had laid out flatbread and cheese. Jori and Ara picked up some food and joined the other children who sat together on the grass near the great fire, eating, laughing, and talking.

As they approached, Kelan looked up. "Where have you two been?" she demanded.

Ara fell to the ground and looked at the older girl. She took a huge bite of cheese, chewed a moment, then opened her mouth wide.

"EWWWW!!!" screeched one of the ducklings as they all looked away.

Ara turned to Jori and winked.

"So, what are you beautiful children up to today?" asked a gnarled old woman who gingerly settled herself on the grass with them.

"We chased butterflies!" Jori said gleefully. "Then Ara and I went for a walk."

Older women often sat with children, close to the fire, helping the smallest with their food and keeping some semblance of order. They all said that their bones liked to be near the warmth. Most of the younger women had to keep to their tasks and carried flatbread with them wherever they worked so they could eat a little from time to time.

Jori looked up from her meal and smiled to see Barde, the Tribe's Singer, join them on the grass. Barde was not yet the age of the Grandmothers, but she did enjoy the company of young ones, and sitting with the children gave her tired feet a brief respite from her day's demands.

This had been a particularly busy day for Barde. One of her duties as Singer was to walk to key points in the village carrying news of the day or messages from the Hearth Queen or the Hunt Queen. Because of tonight's Rite, Barde sang of the reasons for the ritual and its instructions all day long. She also passed on special messages or directions, sometimes secret, to specific people as the occasion demanded. Today, she gave private information to the Cooks regarding the timing of the feast, directing them to bring out the food at a certain point. Barde relayed her precise instructions.

The secrecy of ritual plans was a tradition called "keeping the silence." Garnet explained that the sense of awe and wonder felt by Tribeswomen created an energy force that she could tap into and use in ritual. Spectacularly uninterested in such matters, Jori had not quite understood, but Kelan had. Jori preferred to hunt rabbits with Ara.

Kelan usually absorbed every detail from Barde with great eagerness, and today was no exception. She scooted over to the big woman, trying to look adorable.

"Please, Barde!" Kelan wheedled. "Tell me the ritual plans!"

"Now, Kelan," Barde reasoned, "you know I cannot reveal the Hearth Queen's secrets. She alone decides what is said and to whom. If you must know, ask her yourself."

"I will!" Kelan puffed up self–importantly and ran off.

Barde shook her head, smiling. "I suppose you want to know, too?" she turned to Jori.

"Know what?" Jori looked up from her food, mostly oblivious to the previous conversation. "Oh, no. I guess we will all find out tonight what Mother plans."

"Mmmm, a sensible girl." Barde chewed thoughtfully, "And what are you up to this afternoon?"

"I promised Devin to help her weave a roof for the new grain hut. She and Daña are building three huge huts," Jori said proudly, flinging her arms outward to indicate great size, "and I am helping!"

Barde regarded her little friend thoughtfully. Jori's eyes sparkled like the clear sky whenever she spoke of doing anything with Devin. She was always underfoot, tagging along behind the Hunters. She even made her own bow and arrows and stained them with Devin's colors.

Barde enjoyed the little family of Garnet, Devin, Jori, and Kelan, and she visited them often. If you did not know the girls had different mothers, you would think they were sisters from their demeanor toward one another. Each girl seemed to favor the other's parent, and Barde guessed that, from the way they were brought up, both girls considered both women their mothers. Each daughter simply leaned toward the one whose temperament better matched her own. She shook her head, realizing that she had lost track of what Jori was saying.

"Oh, well then, you had best be off. I walked by the construction a while ago, and they already had the walls up." Barde hoped she sounded like she had been listening.

"Oh, thank you! See you later!" Jori jumped up, brushing crumbs from her chest, and ran off.

Daña tapped on Devin's muscled shoulder and smiled toward the center of the village. From the roof of the new hut, they saw the child winding her way around and toward them. She looked only at the ground and her arms pumped determinedly as she raced headlong across the distance.

"Here comes our little apprentice," Daña chuckled.

"No doubt she is escaping her chores," Devin's deep voice answered. "That child will do anything to get away from Garnet's tasks. I wonder where her little friend is?"

"Ara's mother forbade her to help us build anything; she thinks it is too dangerous."

"Like that would stop Jori!" Devin laughed.

Daña's eyes widened, thinking that Devin was as much a rebel today as she had been when they were small. "Ara is a good girl. She will do as instructed."

"I am glad that Ara still listens to her mother," Devin raised a hand to surrender the point, "but if I forbade Jori from coming here, do you think she would just obey?"

"No. She is too much like you were at her age, always running off to stalk animals or carve tools with or without permission. I seem to remember Norahjen having to track you down a time or two."

"I seem to remember you following right along," Devin grinned. Daña punched her friend playfully and Devin pushed back. Both women laughed as they almost lost their balance.

The child stopped abruptly at the foot of the wall and squinted at them, wondering what was so funny. "May I come up and help you?" she asked, looking hopeful.

"Come on," Devin waved her up, "but be careful of the thatch rows. We have not secured them yet. Stay on the edge."

The girl climbed nimbly to the top of the wall. "Why are you using thatch? Did you not say that when we built our permanent village, you would use wood?"

Devin and Daña exchanged amused glances. "We are not certain that this is our permanent village yet. If enough food grows in the garden and if the winter goes well, next spring we will replace this roof. I will make a bargain with Falcone's Tribe. If the harvest is sufficient, we will trade grain for their help gathering stones and wood for the buildings."

Jori brightened at the mention of her father. "When did you see Falcone? He has not been here yet this year." Devin found her enthusiasm charming.

"They follow herds up the flats, traveling to the foothills. We met them on our last hunt and told them of our new village." The encounter had been simultaneously pleasant and unpleasant. Devin was always glad to see her men friends, but she did not care much for Falcone. His pompous arrogance annoyed her. Still, as Hunt Queen, it was her job to ensure good relations with other tribes.

The men and women had been genuinely glad to see each other. They chatted and laughed together easily, sharing stories about the season's hunting trips and recent travels, until someone asked about Garnet's garden. The friendly talk ceased and Falcone became sarcastic and derisive. Devin stayed positive and cheerful as best she could, and others tried to steer the conversation elsewhere, but the tone of the visit had changed and there was an unsettled feeling in the air when the men moved on.

"What does Falcone say about our village?" Jori asked again, snapping Devin back to the present.

"Let me just say that the men will wait and see what comes up in the fall before they believe in the garden," Devin said dryly.

"Is Toban well?" Toban was her brother who began traveling with the men two summers ago. The Tribe had held a feast to commemorate Toban's change in status, and the celebration lasted two days.

Devin remembered the brave face that Garnet wore for Tobin's benefit and how her attitude helped the boy leave the women with joy. No one but Devin knew her sadness at his departure.

"He has grown tall like a tree. He looks tanned and seems healthy," Daña interjected, tying another bundle of thatch. "You will see him yourself soon enough. They will visit after they have settled."

"They probably want some cheese," Jori offered. The men's Tribe traditionally made a gift of goat's milk when they visited the women, and the women in turn made cheeses that they shared with the men.

"And a good batch Wren has made, too," Devin winked.

"May I go on the next hunt?" Jori asked the Hunt Queen.

"Ask your mother," Devin answered quickly, earning a smirk from Daña. "Now, catch this and attach it to the frame."

Devin tossed the end of the bundle to the child who quickly tied it to the pole frame. She is a natural builder, Devin thought. Too bad Kelan didn't show much interest in this work. She wondered if they had indulged Jori too much, teaching her to track, shoot, and build. She might face a hard transition this fall when her adult training for the role of Hearth Queen began.

Both girls would certainly be happier if they could trade places, but the Elders were already asking about their training and did not seem inclined to allow a change in tradition, even though tradition limited the girls' choices.

Devin believed that handing down the Queens' positions to the daughters was essentially a good tradition. After all, it took a lifetime to prepare for such a pivotal role in the Tribe. But she also believed that traditions were meant to be beneficial guides, not intractable rules.

Devin thought that the elders should be able to see that this situation was different from any other time before. Never before had a Hearth Queen and a Hunt Queen raised their daughters so closely together, as one family. Devin sighed her resolve to simply have faith in the outcome. The collective Tribe was wise, and she believed they would make the right decision in the end.

Devin and Garnet's Tribe currently had four Elders, considered most wise due to the sheer number of winters they had survived. On large rolled hides, the Hechtas scratched signs to keep track of winters' passages, and when a woman survived enough of them, the Tribe held a Croning ceremony. From that day on, the Elder was considered a wise one. Devin thought that some women never became wise, no matter how many winters had passed in their lives, but she rarely shared that view with anyone besides Garnet.

Decisions affecting the whole Tribe were made together. The Tribeswomen gathered and talked through their different views until they agreed upon a plan. Elders always spoke first and last, their opinions highly prized and carefully considered. Devin remembered with pride her own grandmother, Zuza, a very wise woman who lived until Devin was well into her apprentice years.

Zuza had been Hunt Queen as Devin was now, but Devin had never really known her as such. When Devin was only little, her own mother became Hunt Queen, and for most of Devin's life, Zuza kept her sleeping robes among the Hechtas, next to Norahjen, the eldest Scout.

The two women took Devin, Tem, and Daña on many hunting and scouting trips. It was Zuza who first allowed Devin to lead a hunting party, and it was she who taught Devin how to befriend a young dog that came wagging its tail up to camp. Zuza described how dogs live and think about the world, explaining that if you knew the customs of any creature, you could understand it, and if you understood, you could communicate with any animal.

Devin often thought of Zuza when she faced a difficult decision. If she closed her eyes and opened her heart, sometimes she heard Zuza's voice, and many times, her grandmother's advice made a decision easier.

Devin smiled as she remembered how women at the Summer Gathering had called her grandmother "Z" because they could not pronounce her full name, Zuszansuskhanna. Even in the Tribe she was called just Zuza. The family joke was that, while everyone in the Tribe COULD pronounce her name, no one had enough time to do so.

Devin wished her grandmother were still on this earth when the Tribe discussed Garnet's ideas — especially planting seeds and building a permanent village. The battle over the garden had been enormous. Shayana the eldest had argued herself blue, saying she knew the one, true way that the Tribe should live, the way it had always lived, and that any variance would lead only to disaster. A prime example of a woman living long and learning little, Devin thought unkindly.

Two other Elders spoke against Garnet's plan, saying they

did not believe for an instant that she could make food grow where the Tribe wanted to live. They only conceded after the rest of the Tribe expressed faith in Garnet's leadership. Devin and Garnet had thought the meeting was interminable.

Devin shuddered, thinking how difficult it could have been if the Tribe had not supported them. The Tribeswomen followed the Hunt Queen and the Hearth Queen by their own choice. If the argument had gone against Garnet's ideas, the Tribeswomen could have also decided that Garnet and Devin were no longer fit to lead and could have chosen two others as Queens. As faithful followers themselves of the Tribe's will, Garnet and Devin would have respected the decision and followed whomever the women chose, but Devin was happy it had not come to that, and she was grateful for the trust the women placed in their vision.

Even so, they had only given conditional acceptance, which was why Devin used thatch and poles for these buildings. She could not invest the Tribe's resources in extra labor to cut wood and haul stone until she knew they would definitely stay here.

Devin had also agreed to gather as much food as possible for storage in case Garnet's planting bore an insufficient harvest. That way the Tribe would still have plenty for the winter and could pick up and travel again in the spring if need be. If the seeds did grow, the Tribe could trade any surplus food for labor, tools, and other goods.

One turn of the seasons was not very long to test Garnet's plan, but it was all they could coax from the women. Devin closed her eyes for a moment and touched her amulet, sending requests to The Mother for their plan to work. She breathed slowly, worrying the stone gently with her thumb. The amulet was very old, a little carving of The Mother, passed down from Hunt Queen to Hunt Queen and worn almost smooth from rubbing.

Devin dreamed of building a village as a monument to the

ancestors, and she had many ideas to make their home more comfortable and beautiful for everyone. Several winters ago she had visited a desert Tribe that had built a water delivery system to bring the precious liquid from far away. She sketched a diagram onto a hide of the pathways these people had dug for the water to flow through. They lined the canals with stone, and where the water had to flow under the ground, the Tribe dug trenches and laid in fired clay tubes. Water flowed through these tubes into the Tribe's very houses! Devin had other ideas she had dreamed up during several winters' quiet days and nights; the indoor hearth, the stone well.

She learned so much when Hunters met at the Summer Gathering of the Tribes. She was very curious about different ways that others did things, and she wanted to use all that she learned to enhance the life of her Tribe. She envisioned a sturdy village that would be safe in any weather. If Garnet's plan succeeded, Devin's Hunters could spend less time scouting and foraging and more time building wonderful and useful things. Devin smiled at the thought.

By sunset, they finished thatching the roof of the first storage building. When Jori stepped inside, she was amazed at the hut's sheer size. Devin had designed the building with two wings coming out from the center, each large enough to hold up to four drags of food. Drags were customarily made from the hide of an elk or reindeer, folded over long poles, and secured to the poles with sinews. The Tribe used drags to carry everything from people to grains over long distances.

The new building's central area was large enough for two large work tables. Poles across the ceiling could hold enough dried herbs or meats to feed the whole village! And Devin planned two more buildings.

Devin was cleaning herself and her tools at the firepit when Jori joined her there. "Devin, why do we need three big huts? The one we just finished is huge! Is it not enough?"

"There are several reasons," Devin said, giving the child her full attention. "We have learned from our friends at Gatherings that it is not good to store meat and grain in the same building, so we need a different storage hut for each. The meat hut will have a hearth fire in the center so we can preserve meat for winter. Smoke and salt from the meat can damage grain if it is close by."

"A hearth fire? Inside the building?" Jori searched Devin's face, looking for a smile or chuckle, as this was surely a joke. When Devin stayed serious, Jori asked more questions. "How will you keep the smoke from filling the house?"

"We put a hole in the roof, at the center."

"But will snow and rain fall through the hole?"

"Do not worry. We will build a little platform over the hole on the outside. The smoke will go out the sides, and no rain or snow will fall in," Devin explained, beginning to weary of the rapid–fire questions after a long day's hard work.

"Why will we build a third house?" Jori asked her, squinting in concentration.

"To store fruits and nuts and to give us a place to grind grain into flour."

"Grind grain inside?" Jori asked. "Why would we do that?"

"We need an inside place for winter, as you cannot grind grain in rain or snow. If we stay here, an indoor grinding area will let us bake fresh bread all winter long. Now, run off to wash, and then go see your mother to help prepare for ritual. You have neglected her enough for one day," Devin directed.

The child had so many questions! Norahjen swore that smarter children were harder to raise, and Devin understood as she watched Jori grow up. But these lessons were important. She would go over them all again soon to be sure the child remembered.

"Yes, Devin. I'll go to Mother as soon as I clean myself," Jori answered mechanically, then ran off to the washing place.

Devin crossed muscled arms over her small breasts and watched Jori sprint away.

"She really is like you, you know," her friend's voice said behind her.

"I wish my own daughter were more like me," Devin mused, watching where Jori had run off.

"You surprise me!" Looking like a smaller, darker version of the Hunt Queen, Daña stood next to Devin in the same pose. "You raised those girls together, did you not?"

Devin glanced at her and then back to the village. "Yes..." she squirmed a little, trying not to let her discomfort show.

"And both of you always treat them both as your daughters, do you not?" When Daña believed she was right, she was relentless. Devin sighed.

"SO?" Devin dropped her arms and looked squarely at Daña.

"So, Jori is as much your daughter as Kelan is, and both belong to Garnet as well. They think of you both as their mothers; they simply follow the path of the one whose temperament most closely matches their own."

Devin's square face split into a grin. She patted Daña firmly on one shoulder, laughing, "Of course!! I DO have a daughter who follows my path! You are truly wise, my friend!"

Daña shrugged and rolled her eyes. "A blind woman can see that both girls belong to both of you."

"Of course. I forgot Trooper's first lesson," she admitted, still smiling at herself and shaking her head. "Trooper" was the Scout Norahjen's nickname.

"Never stick your hand in the fire?" Daña teased.

"No."

"Never swim in the river by yourself?"

"Nope."

"Always listen to your grandmother even when you do not understand why?"

"Nope."

"Then, what?"

"The very first scouting lesson: Always look right in front of you before you scan the horizon," Devin said.

"Ah, yes. This answer has been in front of you all the time!" Daña smiled at her friend. She knew that Devin was preoccupied with concerns about the girls' eventual paths. To Daña, the answer was simple and obvious: Let the girls follow the paths revealed by their natural talents. But the Elders and others resisted any change in tradition.

"It was," Devin's face fell into a serious scowl. "Now all we have to do is show the Elders the answer that is right in front of us all."

"Yes," Daña considered. "Do not worry," she placed her hand reassuringly on Devin's back. "We will find a way. All will be well."

Shaking the water off her washed arms, Jori closed her eyes and breathed the savory air deeply, considering all of Devin's new plans. She had trouble imagining that next winter they might actually cook and grind grain inside buildings.

As she walked home, Jori thought admiringly of Devin's vision and skill. No one else imagined these wonderful ways to help the Tribe!

Smells of roasted meats and kartof wafted through the entire village; the Hunters had provided well for this feast. The main meal was not to be served until the ritual was underway, so Cooks left out cheese, bread, and fruit for those who needed something to hold them over.

Jori admired the Cooks' many skills, and she stopped

behind a clay oven to watch the bustle of activity. Cooks were organized into several small groups, each with a leader and a specific task. Some washed vegetables for roasting and put them on sticks; some kneaded bread for baking. One apprentice supervised the two dogs Devin had trained to turn spits for roasting meat.

Jori thought perhaps it was no more a miracle to predict where food would grow than it was to train animals to help with cooking. At first, no one believed Devin could get the dogs to do it, but with time and patience, she had. Maybe her mother was also right about food growing from planted seeds, Jori reasoned.

She walked past the serving area, grabbing a handful of raisins and a hunk of cheese. She sat with her back against the side of a hut in the shade and munched contentedly. She loved to watch the life of her Tribe, and sometimes she wished she could fly above the village like a bird so she could see everyone at the same time. She never forgot the first time the old Scout took her up on a high cliff to see the vista of her people and the surrounding lands.

Jori was always aware of the energy in the village, too, and she wondered if Mama's practices had sunk in just a little. Today, women seemed happy and expectant, probably looking forward to the feast and the dancing and wine that would follow. Or maybe moods were high just because spring had finally come after a hard winter.

The children were all very active, some chasing others around the village playing hide–and–find. Children always seemed more boisterous before an important event like a ritual.

Finishing her snack, Jori started home. Mother expected her soon.

"Mama!" she called, approaching the little house they shared.

"Ah, there you are, my love," Garnet scooped the girl up into a hug. "Have you been helping build the storage house?"

"We finished one today. It is huge!" the girl said excitedly. You could fit . . ." she looked around their home, considering, then looked at her fingers and held up four, ". . . you could fit four of our houses into this one hut!"

"My!" Garnet's eyes twinkled in amusement. "That IS large! If we fill those big houses with food, surely we will never go hungry! Now go shake out your sleeping fur," she directed, "and lay it out so the wind freshens it. Then get ready for the ritual. Do you know what to do tonight?"

"Yes, Mother," Jori sighed, rolling her eyes, "I remember. We already practiced it."

The girl picked up her sleeping fur and ran out the door.

Garnet chuckled, shaking her head, and turned to finish dressing.

The cool night air raised bumps on her arms as Garnet stood motionless. The sun was setting now, and this early in the spring, the evening air still held a chill. Once sure that Jori was ready, Garnet went to the woods to prepare herself for the ritual. She could return home for another robe to ward off the chill, but she knew she would warm as soon as she moved around the big circle.

She pushed aside the temporary physical discomfort and concentrated on the life energy that surrounded her. Even during this time of year when the veil between the worlds was thick, Garnet felt her ancestors coming 'round to support her. She held out her hands, palms up, to absorb the energy.

She glanced at the moon's sliver in the sky. Brand new it was, and pale, a good night for 'majikal' planting. She had timed the completion of planting seeds for this moon phase.

Garnet closed her eyes and focused on her dream of crops rising from the fields. Breathing deeply and slowly, she saw tall, golden grains waving in an autumn sun. The vision grew until it banished any doubt, until she believed with certainty what would come to be. Engulfed by the vision and the gathering energy, she swayed.

Opening her eyes, she heard the drums. They could not have been playing long; the heartbeat rhythm was still quiet, as it always was at first. Petrov, the Drum Leader, possessed a skill for managing energy in subtle ways. As Tribeswomen assembled, the drums slowly grew louder and more insistent, pulling all the women's heartbeats into one.

The drums raised their energy to a level where Garnet could shape it and create a vision of her dreams that all could see and believe. This was her job and she was good at it. Her mother told her many winters ago that if the entire Tribe believed something, it was so. Through all time, Hearth Queens believed that each woman creates her own reality, and that was Garnet's dream with the seeds, to create a new reality. The drums beat louder and Devin's whistle pierced the distance, signaling Garnet that it was time for her entrance.

She gathered her robes about her, creating a hood from the excess, and walked slowly to the village center. Four Hechtas appeared as if out of the trees; Garnet was not startled, as she was accustomed to these women's silent comings and goings.

Carrying the sacred tools of Garnet's office, the Hechtas fell into line behind her, their steps matching the stately, slow drumbeat. Herta carried the chalice; Astaga, the torch; Marjika and Nita each carried a basket. The chalice and the stone torch had been handed down through countless generations. No one alive knew exactly how many; not even Herta, The Rememberer, nor Astaga, the Keeper of the Tools.

Garnet's movements were practiced and dramatic. Focusing intently on her message, she slipped into an altered state and felt her conscious mind let go as she floated above the circle. She grew larger, wiser, and more beautiful.

As she stepped into the circle, the drumbeat stopped. She strode to the center, where wood for a bonfire waited to be lit. She took the chalice from Herta and held it up in front of her, focusing on the image of the Great Bear Mother carved into its face. Garnet felt the warmth of Her presence, the softness of Her fur. Lifting the chalice high above her head, she walked around inside the circle, sun–wise.

"Bless thee, oh ancestors who gather with us this night! I call you all to the circle and ask you to assist in our quest! Mothers of our mothers of our mothers, stand with us." She felt the energies gathering around her. "Help us build a home where our children are happy and your spirit is honored." She sipped from the chalice and handed it back to its Keeper.

She turned to Astaga, who dipped the head of the torch toward her. Passing her hands over the cold torch three times, Garnet performed a little 'majik' known only to her and Devin, and the torch–head burst into flame.

As always, the crowd collectively Ahhh–ed. No matter how many times she did this, women always seemed surprised and this made Garnet smile inside. The essence of 'majik' was the belief, and she appreciated the strong faith the women of the Tribe had in her.

Garnet took the flaming torch from Astaga and walked sun–wise around the circle again, absorbing the shining energy from her Tribeswomen. Their warmth filled her.

"Bless thee, oh Mothers! Keep our fires burning, the fires in our hearts and the fires in our hearth! Help us stay warm and healthy this night and all nights that follow!"

Returning to her starting point, Garnet held the torch to a small pile of dried grass at the base of the wood pile, and it roared to life with a whoosh, flaming taller than Garnet in seconds. Standing with her arms raised to the sky and beholding the fire's beauty, she looked through the flames and nodded softly to Devin, who had built this impressive bonfire. Garnet thanked The Mother for Devin, on whom she could always depend. She handed the torch to its Keeper, Astaga, who stubbed out the flame in the sand and retreated.

Closing her eyes now, Garnet felt the intense blend of energies she had gathered. She stirred the energies gently with great love, blending all the glittering flavors into one powerful force. She turned her palms to one another, fingers extended, and felt the energy shape and compress between her hands. She filled the energy ball with her vision for the Tribe.

Opening her eyes, she looked into the dark sky, bent her knees slightly, and suddenly pushed the ball of energy upward, letting it go. She held up her hands, watching the iridescent ball rise and spread its energy into the night sky, then rain down across the village like glittering snow.

Garnet walked around the circle once more, looking each woman and child in the eye. All heard her voice, yet she spoke gently and melodically. "We celebrate our first planting. We come together to ask the ancestors for help to grow these plants into a harvest, a harvest which will help us create our dream: a home to stay in winter and summer, spring and fall. This day, I planted seeds that will grow into grain and vegetables, but they will also grow more. They will give us the means to have a village where we can create, learn, and live all of our days."

Garnet gave a subtle hand signal as she completed the circle. The Hechtas brought baskets to the circle and gave one to Jori and one to Kelan. Jori entered the circle carrying a basket of seeds; Kelan followed with a basket of small pouches.

Marjika stepped forward and led the girls around the circle, taking a pouch from Kelan's basket and putting into it a handful of seeds from Jori's basket. She handed the filled pouch to one woman in the circle and moved to the next. Garnet believed it was important to give ritual participants a remembrance in exchange for the life–force energy they contributed to the 'majik'.

Garnet continued to speak, walking slowly around the fire

and looking into the eyes of each Tribeswoman one by one. "Each of you carries seeds of the life we envision for our people. You carry them in your minds and hearts, in your own visions for our new home. Take this pouch with seeds from this first planting as a reminder of your vision. Please wear the pouch or store it someplace special. Whatever you do, keep this pouch safe and honor it, as you honor the ideas we have agreed upon. We planted not just food today, but also a new way of life for us all. We spent many hours in Council considering what we wanted to build here. Today is the day that our dreams become real!"

As she said the last, she turned to the fire and threw her hands skyward. The fire surged and crackled with unusual colors, seemingly in response to her voice. Garnet stood to savor the effects, then said, "In thanks and honor to our ancestors, we now rejoice and feast, for all acts of love and joy show honor to The Mother. We honor Her gifts as we savor them. Please enjoy the feast. Sing, dance, and enjoy our abundance. May it ever be so."

"May it ever be so!" the women responded vigorously.

To Garnet's ear, they sounded uplifted. She walked from the circle into the darkness beyond the bonfire's glow, and the Hechtas followed, ending the ritual. As was their custom, the Hechtas took the relics back to the Temple to clean, bless, and store.

Garnet walked into the woods to ground herself and return fully to the present. She had found that she could not go directly to the feast because she needed time to shake off the feeling of being in a 'majikal' place.

She bent down, palms to the earth, legs straight, and held the position a few moments, feeling the last of the 'majikal' energy draining into the earth. "Thank you, Mother. I return to you that which I have not used so that another may draw upon it, for the good of all." She spoke the traditional energy—returning words softly, remembering all things that come from The Mother return to Her in time.

As Garnet walked silently to the Temple, she smiled as she heard the first stirrings of the feast in the distance. Over many seasons she had developed a keen ear for her Tribe's mood. Tonight, the women and children sounded confident and happy. It was a good night for a long celebration, and she was anxious to join the fun. She had only a few moments more of duty.

Suddenly in the darkness, she spotted Devin leaning against a tree. Garnet embraced her partner warmly. "Thank you, dear heart, for your fire 'majik'. Your creation was superb."

"I am happy to serve," Devin bowed slightly, grinning. "You were wonderful. I could feel the energy trembling through each woman, except maybe Shayana. She is such a skeptic and absolutely head–blind! She could not feel 'majikal' energy if it swallowed her!"

"Let us not worry about THAT one, darling," Garnet laid her head on Devin's strong shoulder. "I will look in on the Hechtas and then join you at the feast. Have you seen the girls?"

"I saw Jori. She is at the table already," Devin chuckled, kissing Garnet's hair, "and eating as if she will never see another morsel!"

"That is my girl," Garnet laughed. "I do not know where she puts it all. Seems to do her no harm, though."

"She uses a lot of energy chasing Hunters around," Devin said. "She worked all afternoon with Daña and me. Climbs like a squirrel. Ah, well. I will see you at the feast, then." She kissed Garnet quickly. "Do not be too long. You still owe me a dance from the last moon!"

"I thought I paid that debt off in other ways!" Garnet laughed, eyes glittering as she looked at her lover. "You said we were even, remember? But I will dance with you nonetheless if you are worthy."

"That, my love," Devin returned the grin, "is my life's work. I strive always to be worthy of you." Devin kissed her once more and ambled off to the feast.

Watching her back, Garnet warmed. Not every generation of Hunt Queen and Hearth Queen became partners in the manner that she and Devin had, with bonds both spiritual and romantic.

She smiled when she thought of the starry night they first became lovers. She had joined Devin on a walk away from camp, telling the Elders they sought night–blooming plants for ritual.

Their attraction was neither sudden nor impulsive. In fact, Garnet resisted her feelings for some time, but Devin's steady manner and infectious smile finally wore down her reserve. The flowers that Devin picked and brought her almost daily helped, too.

Garnet remembered how that wonderful first night with Devin was unlike anything else she had ever experienced, and after that, she lost all interest in lying with anyone else, including men. Garnet did not know whether it was her bond with Devin that caused her to feel so or if it came from loving women in general. Neither she nor Devin had ever taken another lover, and that, too, was unusual. Some animals paired for life but most humans did not, and Garnet knew that she and Devin were blessed with a very special bond.

Garnet walked to the small Temple. From here it looked like any other house, at least when she looked only with her eyes. Placed in a small stand of fruit trees, the Temple stood away from the rest of the village, the approach to its door decorated with painted symbols, flowers, and herbs. Little pipes strung on branches of trees around the building made sweet musical sounds when the wind spoke through them. In front of the Temple was a fire circle.

This was the one building in the village always intended to be permanent, and it was built first. The entire Tribe slept here through the first rainstorm. It was crowded, but fun, too. Even if the Tribe decided to take the village apart and travel again next spring, the Temple would remain, and they would visit it when their route brought them back here each spring. The Hechtas declared this: Once something was built and dedicated to The Mother, it stayed standing. If the women moved on, this building alone would remain, available to anyone who needed shelter.

Garnet saw a small fire crackling through the trees and could see the Hechtas, cleaning and blessing the ritual tools. Marjika looked up from her work as Garnet approached. The Hechtas all gathered round her as she walked up with her arms outstretched.

"A wonderful rite, my friends!" Garnet said happily, kissing each woman. "You were perfect, as always. Are you all happy with the work?"

"Well, there was the one usual cold spot in the circle," Petrov said in a low, rumbling voice similar in timbre to her big drum, "but we bridged it before anyone else noticed."

"Yes, so Devin said," Garnet smiled. "That is not unusual though. I suppose every generation has one who is heart–blind or just closed. I wish for her sake she were happier, but she is who she is. Thank you for bridging the gap. Are you done with the tools?"

"Astaga is finishing now. We were about to have a cup of wine." Marjika held up her own cup. "Will you join us?"

"In a moment," Garnet said, stepping into the warm and softly lit Temple.

Astaga stood next to the altar, wiping the chalice with a small, pliable skin. She did not look to see who had entered; many years of service told her the answer.

The old stone torch stood, its end secured in a large pot of earth, its flame creating shadows over the old woman's craggy features. The flame's flickers told Astaga that she would soon have to replace the torch's head, one of her responsibilities as Keeper of the Relics.

She swaddled the chalice with fur, carefully placed it on the altar of wood and stone, and turned her attention to Garnet.

"You have built a beautiful altar for the relics. You must have spent days rubbing fat into the wood to get it to gleam so!" Garnet complimented her.

Astaga nodded her thanks and gently laid her hand on the roll of hide near the chalice that contained the birth and death records of the tribe. Symbols pressed into the leather held considerable information for those who knew how to read them.

"I wanted to create a place for our tools and other special relics that reflects their beauty, like the hide bags, only permanent, like our new home. I have an idea of something different to build during the summer."

Up to this time, relics had always been wrapped in furs and stored in hide bags. When the Tribe traveled, Astaga's duty was to pull the drag with the relics. Sometimes others helped over rough ground or across mud and rivers, but most often, she pulled the drag herself, a leather strap slung across her broad shoulders. Garnet wondered what she had in mind now for the precious tools.

"Tell me?" Garnet prodded. Astaga always voiced her ideas reluctantly, and Garnet did not know if the big woman was unsure of herself or simply shy.

"Well, I want to find a small tree, about my height with a few low branches. I want to...what do you call it? Plant it, here, in the middle of the room. After the tree has lived here a season or two and its roots have grown in this space, I will place the relics in the crooks of its branches. I want to ask women of the Tribe to carve symbols into the bark, and Herta wants to hang her teaching scrolls from the tree as well. Devin says she can build a roof that will allow the tree to grow without letting the rain and snow in."

"That is a fine idea!" Garnet exclaimed. "Have you selected a tree yet?"

"Oh, no," Astaga laughed. "We all will be involved in that, but I am keeping my eyes open. We do not want to begin until next season, anyway."

Garnet was enthralled. "What ever made you think of this?" she asked.

"I learned it from a woman in the Tribe that calls itself the Celts. They honor trees as the embodiment of wisdom. Their beliefs are similar to ours, and their practices are interesting."

Garnet was amazed. Astaga had not talked this much about anything in many winters. She must truly be excited!

Abruptly ending the discussion, Astaga turned toward the door. "Now, for that cup of wine?"

Garnet looked around the Temple room. It was not as large as the new storage huts, but it held several people comfortably. A stack of furs sat in one corner and baskets of herbs in another. Garnet smelled comfrey and mint. Stumps for sitting lined one wall.

Women came and went from the Temple regularly. The Hechtas used the space as a workroom during inclement weather, and many Tribeswomen came often to work, to seek counsel, or just to sit. It was a truly communal home, a room of quiet and peace.

Garnet took a deep breath and exhaled. She stepped into the cool evening behind the Keeper of the Tools, sat in a place the others had saved for her near the fire, and took a cup of wine offered by Petrov.

Wine was one of the special 'majiks' of the Hechtas, who produced and protected it. Garnet got a chill thinking how dangerous the effects of wine could be when it was outside the control of the ritualists. Some who enjoyed wine on feast days were seduced by the pleasant feelings, and those without the discipline of 'majikal' training sometimes used it too often or without thought to the consequences. The mirth produced by wine offered a good release, but it had to be used wisely.

The old ones taught that wine was like certain spiders that lured their lovers with heady intoxication and then ate them as they slept. The Hechtas monitored the use of wine closely and offered it only sparingly.

Still, this was a feast night and even Garnet planned to partake a little. Ever protective of her health, the Hechtas insisted that she, too, relax occasionally, and in moderation, wine helped loosen worry and gave a happy sense of warmth.

"Thank you, Petrov," Garnet said, taking a sip. She smiled with appreciation at Marjika, who had made this batch from plums. At first, it tasted tart on the tongue, then left a lingering sweetness a few moments after the tartness disappeared.

Rhythms of toads and brika bugs combined to make a song of the night. The Hechtas were a quiet group, speaking only when they had something to say. After rituals or other major work, they often just sat looking at the crackling fire and listening to the music of the natural world.

The Hechtas did not attend the regular feast, nor did they often mix with the rest of the Tribe. They built their house within sight of the Temple and preferred to stay close to home.

The Hechtas were keepers and protectors of knowledge and tools. Over many generations, they had also become silent guardians of the physical campsite, roaming the outskirts of the village in pairs, watching for any danger. The Hechtas warned of storms or approaching tribes, and Devin's Scouts often reported to them even before reporting to her. The Hunters thought some Hechtas communicated with animals and birds because they always seemed to know when a large herd was nearby, and once they warned the Tribe of a stampede in time to get everyone out of the way.

Some women were wary of the secretive group; others came to them for guidance and advice. Garnet stayed with the Hechtas one season as part of her training, and she knew their traditions and hearts intimately. She trusted them with her very self. She even knew the name they called themselves, never repeated outside their circle: the born–to's. Hechtas believed that membership in their group was a matter of destiny, not choice. In their eyes, you either were a Hechta or you were not. It was not a path that one chose; the path chose you.

Garnet's lifelong exposure to this special group helped her understand them, and they were fiercely loyal to her. In any crisis or emergency, the Hechtas' first task was to ensure the safety of the Queen, after which they did her bidding and saw to the rest of the Tribe's well being. But, like bees, they looked first to the Queen.

Devin built her own house between the village and the Temple. Scouts often visited the Hunt Queen in the night or very early morning, and she explained to Garnet that concerns for disturbing the Tribeswomen's sleep coupled with her own preference for relative solitude prompted her to build beyond the circle's edge. She chose a site near the Temple because she felt kinship to the Hechtas and relished their company. She also had lived with the Hechtas for several winters when she was younger, and she had been initiated into the group. Her initiation symbol was a tattoo on her left upper arm of three crescents entwined with one another.

Garnet's role as Hearth Queen required her sleeping place to be in the village center so that her Tribemates could find her easily. For her house in this new village, Garnet chose a site between the common hearth and the homes of the Elders. But Garnet also treasured the nights she spent in Devin's house, close to these good women and the Temple. She was also an initiate of the Hechtas and felt great kinship with these women of 'majik'. Their role, Devin's, and her own overlapped and meshed in their combined service to the Tribe, as they all lived in the 'majikal' realm as well as the physical. Garnet was grateful that they shared this strong bond, and she wondered if it had always been so for Hechtas and Queens.

Garnet finished her wine, said good evening, and walked back to the feast. As she approached she heard Barde's beautiful voice, singing a lively tune about an inept Hunter who is outsmarted by a fox. The children laughed uproariously at each verse.

Garnet stopped to scan the scene. Villagers milled around enjoying the evening. Feast tables sat in a long row on one side of the bonfire, heaped with plates of roasted meats, kartof, fruits, and pitchers of sweet plum wine.

Some women played their instruments and drums for dancing on a large, cleared flat area. Some stood and watched the fire or chatted with others. The music drifted on the night air, and sounds of women talking and laughing were heard throughout the village.

At the feast tables, Garnet filled a plate, then found a place and sat down, smiling at those around her. Everyone chatted happily, ate, or danced. The roast was succulent and the kartof was soft in the middle with crispy skin, just as she liked it.

Garnet felt ravenous after a ritual. She ate slowly, remembering the Healers' lessons about over–indulging.

"There you are, darling." Devin dropped down next to her with a casual thud. "How are things at the Temple?"

"Quite fine," she managed to say between mouthfuls. "I stayed for a cup of wine."

"That is only fitting. Did Astaga tell you her idea?"

"Yes, and I love it! Can we do it?"

"Of course." Devin's utter confidence showed in her quick reply.

"Where are Kelan and Jori?" Garnet looked around the table.

Devin used the bird's leg she gnawed to point to a group of children nearby. "There they are, playing hide–and–find with the others. They want to sleep at my house tonight, and I told them they could."

"Mmmmm . . . good." Garnet crunched into crisp kartof skin. "They are always so excited after a ritual. They will be up all night talking."

"I am going hunting in the morning. I will take them along so you can sleep in." Devin reached over and brushed a crumb from her lover's chin.

"Thank you. I welcome the rest," Garnet admitted, tired from her exertions. "Everyone seems happy."

"Yes, this is a most merry night. The wine flows freely, perhaps a little too freely," Devin frowned.

"It is a feast, dear," Garnet said, a little surprised by Devin's disapproving tone. "Besides, there is only so much to go around. Nita only opens one cask at a time, and that is not enough for anyone to over–indulge." Garnet was puzzled by her lover's consistently negative attitude toward wine. Like the Hechtas, she was well aware of its danger, but Garnet believed it was safe enough when used in moderation. Like any other 'majikal' tool, wine was dangerous only if wrongly used.

"Oh, no? Take a look at Shayana."

Garnet scanned the crowd and found the tipsy woman, eyes glassy, sitting at the end of a long table alone, clutching a goblet and swaying. "Oh, my. We must ask someone to take her home. She is too old for this."

"And lacks the sense to stop after she has had a little," Devin's tone was derisive.

"Now, dear, I know she is annoying, but she is not stupid. There must be a reason it affects her so." She spotted one of the Healers. "Anna!"

"Hello, Garnet!" The tall, dark woman approached the

Queen smiling. "Wonderful ritual. Are you having a good time?"

"Yes, but I need your help." Garnet nodded down the table. "Take a look at Shayana, will you?"

"Ah," Anna sighed heavily, "she has gone too far again. She has done that several times since her Croning. We usually just put her to bed. I will speak to the other Healers tomorrow and see if we can do something more. She cannot endanger herself this way at every feast! She has grown too frail for the next morning's headaches."

Anna walked away to find someone to assist her.

"How long has this been going on?" Devin demanded.

"Several seasons now," Garnet shrugged. "It seems her body has lost its capacity to handle wine. It makes sense; her stomach is sensitive to some foods, too. The Healers will take care of her. Come, let us present a merry front to the other women. Dance with me?" She stood and held her hand out to Devin, who took it and rose to follow her partner to the dance ground.

Seeing them approach, Barde switched to a slower song, aware of Garnet's fatigue after rituals. The musician sang a love ballad she had learned many winters before, and women danced closely and swayed to the soothing tune. Garnet laid her head on the Hunt Queen's strong shoulder and smiled contentedly.

In due time, the children drifted off to sleep and Garnet soon followed, but many women stayed late, dancing and singing until the birds announced the dawn.

"Ouch!" Kelan yelped, stepping on another thorn. She swung her fist through the air as tears ran down her cheeks. Why did she have to come on this stupid hunt anyway?

"There, there. Let me see," Devin said softly as she bent to remove the thorn. "It is not a bad puncture, dear. Your foot is fine. Come and look at the thorn plant again."

Jori rolled her eyes at the other Hunters. Kelan was such a pain. Her noise and disruptions would scare off any animals before the Hunters could get within range. This was the third time she had stepped on a thorn!

"See?" Devin moved the flower petals gently aside. "This thorn hid under this other flower. They are crafty. Watch carefully; these are important lessons."

"How can I see a thorn when it hides???" Kelan demanded in an overtired toddler's tone.

"Shhh! You learn to spot them by practice. Come along and watch." Devin turned and whispered, "Jori, lead the party toward the flats. Keep us in the trees and stop near the edge."

Jori nodded and walked away quietly. Devin had called them to silence some time ago. Hunting parties used hand and face signals as much as possible and spoke only when necessary, which helped Scouts avoid noisy distractions and helped ensure that any nearby animals did not hear the Hunters' approach.

Devin took up position in front of Kelan so she could point out thorns until Kelan got the knack of seeing them. Puncture wounds from thorns sometimes turned ugly and caused real trouble, and Kelan already had three of them. Devin wondered why Kelan had such trouble with thorns? Knowing thorns' power and how to avoid being wounded by them were basic lessons that children learned before they were allowed out of the village. But Devin knew that her daughter had no interest in such things, nor in hunting at all for that matter.

This was only Kelan's second hunt; her first time out, they had not found a herd or even any isolated animals of any size.

Devin had debated with the obstinate child a good part of last evening, trying to persuade her that it was the wise choice to make this trip. As bedtime approached, Devin finally just ordered her to come along.

Kelan was capable enough with a tool when she had to be,

but she preferred letting others do certain tasks. It was not that she was not smart or quick; she just had no interest in Devin's skills. On the other hand, she was fascinated with babies and young children, with cooking, and with stories the old ones told around twilight fires. And she seemed to learn Garnet's 'majikal' practices easily.

Devin spotted a large thorn plant and pointed to it. Kelan barely glanced down as she stepped haughtily around it. Devin took the girl's arm and stopped her, pointing down. Kelan looked impatient, then her eyes dutifully followed Devin's point down to the plant. Devin held her there a moment, then let go, and they continued hiking through the woods. Devin sighed at how fiercely Kelan resisted what came so naturally to Jori.

Jori held her hand up in a signal to stop. Devin took in the whole scene, assessing Jori's choice of stopping place right where the trees began to thin. Dappled patches of sunlight spotted the ground and an occasional breeze brushed her bare arms. Devin smiled; Jori chose well. Although it was not obvious to everyone, they were near the edge of the trees.

Devin left Kelan's side and walked silently to the front of the party. She tapped Jori's shoulder three times, signaling that she was taking back leadership.

Devin considered the compact little warrior with natural Hunter's skills. She leaned over and whispered, "Stay near Kelan. Help her." Jori responded with a sour expression, but Devin nodded and her face was stern and unyielding. Jori sighed and crept toward her sister. Devin shook her head ruefully. Were all children so contrary at this age?

She crouched low and led the party slowly toward the trees' edge. The Hunters had to move stealthily now, staying behind trees as much as possible. Devin was proud of her Hunters. Even though they were all around, she heard only small ruffling noises, like wind in the leaves. Following her lead, the

Hunters moved a few steps, then paused, then moved again. They had learned this from watching predatory felines whose movements mimicked the natural gusts and lulls of the winds. If they kept a steady, more human pace, the Hunters alerted their prey and lost their feast.

Hunters moved along the tree line as Devin's eyes scanned for a good place to wait. She sought a small stand of trees close to a clump of high grass, an ideal spot.

Beyond the trees a meadow led down to the river, and animal herds crossed the open area to get to the water. A variety of beasts spent morning hours at the river, playing, bathing, and drinking. Afterwards, they returned to the forest to nap or eat.

Hunters looked for a place where the animals would cross back into the woods. Animals often walked through stands of high grass, nibbling the tender stalks along the way to their nap. When the animals' bellies were filled with cold water and grass, they became less quick and agile, giving Hunters their best chance at a kill.

Seeing a good place, Devin held up her arm for the Hunters to stop and wait. They all found hiding places behind trees or bushes, crouching or sitting in ready positions.

From her vantage point at a stand of scrub bushes, Jori saw a Scout materialize from behind a tree. Scouts were very good at stealth, even better than Devin. They crept across meadows on their bellies, getting close enough to hear the snuffling noises of the animals without scaring them off.

The Scout silently indicated the size of the herd to Devin. Jori could not see all the hand signals, but she saw Devin's face and Devin looked pleased.

The scent of pine needles filled Jori's nostrils and their ends prickled her bottom as she sat on the ground to prepare. She quietly readied her bow. Its grip fit her hand perfectly, and its smooth feel in her palm reassured her. She put the bow on the ground close enough to grab quickly and turned to help Kelan ready her own bow. But Kelan was sitting there drawing in the dirt with a stick, not even paying attention!

Jori sighed with exasperation. Why did they have to bring Kelan along anyway? She hated being here and might make a mistake that cost the party their bounty. The Tribe's custom held that if a hunting party failed to get meat, its members had to gather kartof, lentils, or fruit on the road back so that no party ever returned empty–handed. No sense wasting a walk, the Elders said, but Jori did NOT want to go gathering today.

She touched Kelan on the shoulder and brusquely made the sign to get ready. Kelan huffed and reached for her bow. She readied the string, looking annoyed.

Jori looked back at Devin, whose hand remained in the air, signaling stillness. She would drop her hand when the time came to attack.

Jori sensed approaching animals before she heard them. Her body tensed when she saw the first elk walk into the forest, a small male. His hide was dappled like the sunlight on the forest floor, and he looked neither left nor right as he wandered along.

As he passed close to the girls, Jori held her breath. Kelan shifted her weight and scuffed her toe in the pine needles. The buck stopped suddenly and looked over his shoulder directly at her.

Jori held her bowstring so taut that her bicep burned, and at that moment she let go with a zinging whoosh. The animal dropped to the ground. Jori's heart pounded so loudly she was sure she would scare the rest of the herd, but they did not seem to hear and continued to walk through the tree line until the silence was shattered by Kelan's scream at the sight of the fallen buck. As the rest of the herd scattered, Devin dropped her hand in a signal for all to fire, and Hunters pursued elk in all different directions.

Jori's buck lay still. She had made a perfect shot, killing

it with one arrow. She ran to the animal and touched the soft down on its face as it shuddered in death. She said ritual words of thanks to the animal for its life, words she had learned from the Hunters, who also called animals to them before a hunt with secret rituals. Now that she had made her first kill, Jori could attend those ceremonies, too. She grinned, her heart bursting with joy.

Kelan was frozen to the spot, her mouth agape in horror. "You killed it," she squealed, "with one shot!"

"Of course," Jori's enthusiasm was unhampered, though her sister's shock confused her. "That was the idea. I will go see how the others did, and I will report my kill to Devin. Stay here and sit down. You look pale."

Kelan had seen Hunters bring meat home many times, but by the time carcasses were carried to the village, they had been cleaned and dressed. Seeing a prepared haunch of elk or deer was very different from seeing a living animal suddenly give up its life.

Kelan swallowed hard and sat down. She felt the forest floor spin and tilt at odd angles, as if she were falling from a tree, but she knew she was not. Her heart pounded and her face felt hot. Deep breaths helped calm her a little.

Jori crept through the woods and spotted Tem.

"Tem," Jori said quietly, "where is Devin?"

"She chased one through the thicket. I think it was wounded, and she wanted to be sure it was finished."

Devin never let a wounded animal escape if she could help it. Injured animals that ran off into high brush suffered greatly and eventually died, and Devin thought it kinder to track and kill the animal quickly. This way, the gift of food was not wasted as well.

"Tem, I made a kill. Will you come and see since Devin is not here?" Jori asked the woman.

"You made a kill?" Tem grinned, clapping the young Hunter on the shoulder. "You did not kill a child, did you?"

"Of course not," Jori huffed indignantly as they walked to the downed animal. "I killed a small buck, though he did have his first horns."

When they reached the elk, Tem bent down to inspect. "Good shot!"

Quietly, Jori got Tem's attention and pointed to Kelan, who sat nearby trembling with her eyes closed. "I think she might faint."

Tem walked over and sat next to Kelan, signaling Jori to go away. Jori happily sprinted off to find the other Hunters.

"Kelan?" Tem inquired quietly. "Are you all right?"

Kelan opened her eyes. "I got a little dizzy when I saw . . ." her voice trailed off as she looked at the dead, young buck lying there.

"I understand. This often happens the first time someone sees a kill," Tem patted her shoulder lightly.

"It was just so f–f–fast! Kelan stuttered. "The animal was dead before I could move."

"Come," Tem offered the girl a hand and stood, "we will gather branches to make a drag for Jori. You could use a walk, and you should not see the cleaning process now. It is too soon."

Kelan gratefully took Tem's strong, warm hand, which reminded her of walking with her mother when she was very small. Calm flooded through her palm, and she let out a deep, cleansing breath. The two walked deeper into the woods.

"THE HUNTING PARTY RETURNS WITH MEAT! Come, all, and see!" Barde sang throughout the village.

Women and noise filled the entrance to the hearth circle. All chatted with excitement, straining for a glimpse of the returning Hunters.

Arms folded across her ample chest, Wren stood near the village entrance conferring quietly with Garnet when the hunting party came into view. When the Tribeswomen realized that they pulled not one, but three drags full of meat, all gasped and clapped their hands to welcome the successful Hunters. This party had done very well! Wren happily wondered if they had enough salt to preserve all this meat.

"We bring food, sister," Devin spoke the ritual words to Garnet loudly, bowing low. "The Mother was generous today."

"The Tribe is grateful, my sister." The Hearth Queen turned to Wren, who prepared to accept the meat and announce the feast. Wren was nervous when she had to speak in front of everyone, and when she opened her mouth, at first no sound came out. Garnet smiled kindly and nodded at her. Garnet had once suggested that when Wren felt like this, it was simply a sign from The Mother that this was a moment to savor. Garnet taught her to take a deep, cleansing breath first and then speak.

"We will prepare food for all," Wren said, taking possession of both her voice and the drags. "Our Mother provides well, and we thank the Hunters for their efforts." So far, so good. She turned to Garnet, "We will use these gifts well."

Garnet smiled encouragingly. "We trust your skills, my sister," her silky voice gave the ritual reply.

Wren felt more confident. She bowed and turned to the crowd, raising her voice louder. "We feast this night on fresh meat! Barde will call us together when the food is ready!"

Many hands helped Wren carry the meat into the hearth circle, where large hides had been laid for it near the big fire. Cooking tools and jars of salt sat nearby. An excited buzz of voices rose as the women began preparations for the feast.

These were happy tasks. When a big kill came in, everyone

helped: Some cut the meat, others wrapped it in large leaves and carried it to the Cooks, while still others rubbed it with salt, helped prepare the roasting pit, or prepared other dishes for the feast. Children gathered fuel for the fire and leaves to wrap the meat, or they carried water and tools where told.

It was a busy time, full of laughter and chatter with all hands busy, even those of the oldest and the youngest. Grandmothers walked toddlers around the encampment, gathering moss, leaves, and small stones for the boiling skins. Other Grandmothers watched the youngest children in the big hut where babies played. Each person had a task, and each task contributed in an important way to the Tribe's life.

Wren saw the Hunters prepare for Garnet to lead them to the Temple, where they would present the animals' hooves, antlers, and hides to the Hechtas. The three who had killed elk joined the Queens at the front of the procession, and the rest of the Hunters lined up behind them and they stepped off. Garnet's eyes widened in surprise and her heart leapt when she saw that Jori was one of the three. She wiped a proud tear from her eye.

Garnet felt Devin squeeze her hand; she saw a mixture of pride and worry in Devin's steel blue eyes and wondered at the source of her conflict, knowing Devin would tell her when they were alone.

Approaching the Temple, Barde sang the ritual song. "The hunting party returns with meat. Come and give great thanks!"

The fire circle in front of the Temple crackled with life, dancing flames projecting auras of glowing light and shadow around the waiting Hechtas. They stood all in a line, awaiting the Hunters' procession. Each woman held the symbol or tool of her office, and a long table nearby held pitchers of wine and plates of cheese and bread.

Astaga's eyes twinkled with warmth and pride when her gaze found young Jori.

Marjika's face reflected joy and pride, too, as she addressed the leaders, "We are told you bring us good news, my sisters."

"We bring news of a good hunt," Devin intoned. "We are grateful for the generosity of The Mother and the herd."

"For the record, who made these kills?" Herta asked, leaning over a large hide with a ritual writing tool in her hand.

"The first kill was made by Jori, daughter of Garnet," Devin announced as she motioned Jori forward.

Standing shyly between her two mothers, Jori held up her offering of two small horns and four hooves wrapped in the hide of the recently killed buck. Even at her young age, she had heard the ritual words often enough to need no prompting. She turned to Astaga and offered the bundle, "Please accept these gifts of the hunt and see that they are used well."

Astaga took the bundle from the child, smiling kindly. "Thanks to The Mother for Her gifts," she replied gently.

Usually, she made tools for the great hearth from a hunt's antlers and hooves, then gave the hide to any Tribeswoman who needed a blanket or a garment. But this bundle she set aside. As the first kill of such a young girl, and that girl being who she was, Astaga and the other Hechtas treated this particular gift with special care. The small buck's antlers would be carved and sharpened into knives, and the hooves would be turned into scrapers. The hide would be tanned and sewn into a special robe, and all these gifts would be presented to the child during the ritual of her first moon cycle.

Astaga had to ask Herta to be sure, but she thought perhaps Jori was the youngest member of the Tribe ever to kill an antlered animal. She was a special child indeed; the Hechtas had known this since her birth.

Jori hid behind Garnet, leaning against her mother. She may have killed an elk, but she was still young enough to become shy when she was the center of attention. Garnet put her arm comfortingly around the girl, and they listened as the two other Hunters took their turns offering gifts to the Temple.

Once done, all the Hunters were invited to sit for wine, snacks, and to tell the hunt's stories. Herta and her apprentice listened to them all and added the stories to the great body of the Tribe's knowledge. All stayed near the Temple until the tired Hunters went to the stream together to bathe, after which they returned to their own homes to rest until time for the feast.

Later, Garnet went to Devin's house to share a concern that nagged at her. After she saw that Jori and Kelan were bathed and settled in for naps at her own house, she left them and sought the solace of her mate.

The girls had been quiet and tense as they cleaned themselves. Garnet asked Jori to tell more details of her kill, but the young Hunter seemed reluctant to talk. She said only that she was in the right place at the right time, and the buck was confused and so had come close enough for her to get a clear shot. Kelan did not speak at all.

Garnet entered Devin's house and sat next to her. "So? What really happened out there?"

"I did not see, but Tem tells me that the buck walked right past the hiding girls and turned to stare at them. Jori reacted instantly and got off a perfect shot."

"But why is she not boisterous and bragging?" Garnet was perplexed.

"Kelan screamed when she saw the dying buck. She became pale and trembled, and Tem took her for a walk in the woods to gather poles for a drag while we cleaned and dressed the animal."

"Oh, I see. And Jori thinks if she tells the story of her kill, she will embarrass Kelan. No wonder you looked so worried before," Garnet finished for her. "I do not understand Kelan's reaction. She has seen fresh blood before — we used it when I taught her to scry — and she has seen Hunters bring meat into camp many times."

"But she has never before seen a live animal pass over, darling. That is much more vivid than seeing the results later." Devin put her arm around Garnet, who rested her head comfortably on the big shoulder. "Tem thinks she will get over it in time. She said that Kelan seemed better after they talked."

"Tem is a good friend. It sounds like she handled the situation with sense and tact. I see why you rely on her." Garnet paused and then looked into the blue eyes she held so dear. "What do we do about this?"

"I think we should make little of Kelan's reaction. We must praise Jori for her quick reflexes and good aim. Even though I had not yet given the signal, she made the right choice to shoot when she did or else the buck would have run, from what I heard. I think we should ignore the rest. Tem is right. We must wait and see if this passes. I will take them on another hunt when the moon thins again, and we can see how Kelan does."

"Meanwhile, I will work with them on things that Kelan is good at. That should help her feel more certain of herself and keep Jori's head from swelling. I do have to say I am pleased with Jori's concern for her sister's feelings," Garnet added.

"Did you ever wish . . .?" Devin started, tracing little patterns in the dirt at her feet. "Oh, never mind," she stopped abruptly.

". . . that we could switch daughters?" Garnet laughed, hearing the thought her partner did not express out loud. "I love them both, but you are right. Each would be happier in the robes of the other. Trust in The Mother, dear. Things have a way of working out."

"Do you have something in mind?" Devin peered closely at her lover.

"Nothing specific. I just trust that all will be well, and so should you. Now is the time to rest. It has been a long day for you, too. I must see how Wren is doing. Someone will come for you when the feast is ready."

Garnet kissed Devin deeply. A familiar tingling sensation traveled up her spine and made her wish she could join the tired Hunter in bed, but she left and walked to the center of the village.

Devin lay on her sleeping furs thinking about the children, supposing that Garnet was right. The Mother resolved life's puzzles in ways that were best for everyone, and the girls' training did not start for a while. There was still time.

The cooking circle was a beehive of activity, with everyone engaged in some task or other. Wren seemed to be everywhere at once, adjusting the spit on which the haunch roasted, admonishing girls to keep the dogs moving at a steady pace, and checking on the salting and wrapping of the surplus meat. Garnet smiled appreciating Wren's considerable skills as she approached the Cook.

"Greetings, Garnet. I have been wondering — do you think it is all right to have meat again so soon after another feast?" Wren asked.

"It is unusual, but it seems ungrateful to forego a roast on a day the Hunters have had such luck. I will ask one of our Healers, though, if you wish." Garnet assured her, "I am sure they know the answer."

"That will ease my mind," Wren admitted.

Garnet nodded and left for the home of Lia. She tapped at the doorway and waited politely.

Lia opened the door and smiled with eyes beaming at the Hearth Queen. "Hello, Garnet. I was just thinking of you. Come and sit, and tell me why you bless me with your presence." The little woman guided Garnet to an area where three stools waited.

Garnet sat and folded her hands carefully in her lap. She

was never completely comfortable in Lia's presence, as Lia had made numerous romantic overtures toward her. She always tactfully refused the Healer but Lia seemed undeterred, and though she was respectful of Garnet's feelings, she made it clear that she remained very interested.

Garnet had no interest in lying with Lia. Not that she was undesirable, but Garnet was simply not attracted to her as a bed partner and she told Lia so. Lia persisted out of a fervent belief that Garnet's feelings might change over time.

"I came to ask about dinner," Garnet explained. "We just had a feast last evening with several kinds of meat. Today, the Hunters returned with elk, so, of course, the Cooks are roasting part of the kill. Do you foresee any trouble for anyone? Is it all right to eat so much of something as strong as meat? Wren is particularly concerned."

"A good question," Lia smiled at her. "I think it is fine, except for those who always have trouble with meat and possibly for some of the Elders with sensitive bellies. I suggest that the Cooks not serve it again for a few days. Eating the same food for an extended time is not good. Balance and moderation are the keys. We should always have a mix of foods as best we can, depending on the season and the hunt."

"Thank you, Lia. I will tell Wren not to worry," Garnet rose to leave.

"Ah, but can you not visit for awhile?" Lia asked wistfully, taking Garnet's wrist.

"I am afraid not," Garnet smiled, extricating her hand from the woman's grasp and edging to the door. "Many tasks await."

She exited with as much dignity as possible and went to find Wren.

Two days later, Garnet sat in the warm sun with Kelan and Jori in front of her house as the girls sang the Animal Song.

Barde had devised several teaching songs for children, easy–to–remember tunes with basic information about the Tribe and its surroundings. Garnet thought songs could help children learn the basics and prepare them for eventual entry into formal instruction, and it was good practice for their tenth winter, when they would begin their apprenticeships. The Tribe used songs to teach apprentices complicated recipes, travel routes, and other critical information for their trades. Melodies made the lessons easier to remember.

In the lives of most children, learning these songs was a casual activity, but for the daughters of the Hearth and Hunt Queens, it was essential. Garnet smiled as she watched her girls. Kelan knew all the songs word–for–word and loved to sing them. Jori fidgeted, hemmed, hawed, and sang a few words in intermittent bursts.

The Animal Song recounted the names and basic attributes of several animals in the Tribe's world, as well as some of the mystical qualities associated with each. They had been singing for some time and were almost at the end.

Kelan sang in her warbling soprano,

"Honor all who walk the earth;
Thank them for the gifts they give;
Warmth and food and health and knowledge;
The Mother blesses all who live.

Hail to thee, oh mighty reindeer,
Who gives us meat and so much more.
You help us find the food that keeps us
Even under fields of snow.

Hail to thee, the little foxes;
Small you are, but quick and smart.
You build a den under the thick brush,
And keep your cubs close to your heart."

Garnet held up her hand to stop the girl. "When do the Hunters bring in foxes?"

"Only after midsummer!" Jori jumped in.

"Why?" Garnet chuckled. Jori did know about hunting.

"Because before midsummer female foxes might be pregnant or nursing their cubs, but when midsummer comes, their children have been weaned. We must be careful not to kill pregnant or nursing mother foxes, or one day there will be no more foxes for us to hunt at all!"

"What do we get from foxes?" Garnet asked her.

"We use the fur for mittens…" Jori began.

". . . and sometimes bags for babies," Kelan interrupted, "and you use the blood for scrying."

"Excellent," Garnet said. "Jori, sing the next section."

Jori began begrudgingly.

> "Hail to thee, our Great Bear Mother;
> Who is our ally and our guide.
> We will never hunt your children
> For you protect and teach our Tribe."

"Well done, even if lacking in enthusiasm," Garnet's gentle voice admonished lightly. "What does this verse mean? Why do we never hunt Bears?" She shot a quelling look at Kelan to silence her mid–word. "Jori?"

"The Great Bear teaches our Queens about herbs, foods, and healing, and in return we promise not to hunt Her Tribe."

"Who is this Great Bear?" Garnet pressed, as this part of the song was very important.

"She is The Mother in the form of a large She–Bear. She appeared to our ancestor, Jorana, when the Tribe was sick with the plague and showed her the remedy."

"Correct. Remember, you are named for Jorana," Garnet smiled.

"But Mother, why does Falcone's Tribe hunt Bears?" Jori asked. "Does this not anger the Great Bear Mother?"

"Each Tribe has its own ways, dear," Garnet held her voice calm. This was an important moment, she knew, and a chance to reinforce the Tribe's most sacred belief: the right to choice. "We share our information with other tribes, but we do not interfere in their practices or customs. We accept each as it is."

"I am sad that men do not know the wisdom of the Great Bear Mother," Kelan frowned, trying to look wise.

"They have their own ways to contact The Mother, dear. Falcone says that his Tribe does not kill the Toad because they revere it as Her messenger. The Mother is with us all, no matter how we contact Her."

She kept the girls with her all morning until even the eager Kelan showed signs of restlessness. "Go now and eat something, my dears. There are other things I must also do today." She kissed both girls lightly on their foreheads as they departed.

Garnet, too, felt restless and walked to the edge of the encampment. A walk let her stretch out tired muscles, and the solitude gave her a chance to breathe. She had been busy lately, working to bring the hearts of her Tribeswomen together behind her vision. She felt as if she had talked for seasons, and she chuckled, thinking that maybe she had.

She and Devin had discussed the idea of a permanent village ever since Garnet could remember. Smiling, she thought of their once youthful enthusiasm and impatience. Many seasons had passed as they developed all their plans, and during those seasons she worked with seeds and plants, learning how they grow and trying to get them to grow in certain places. She planted seeds, marked the spot, and then checked the next time the Tribe went through the area to see if and how well plants grew. It took several seasons more to convince the Tribeswomen that her plan would work.

Lost in her thoughts, she did not notice swarms of butterflies slowly drifting away as she walked, parting before her like mist scattered by a sunbeam. Occasionally she unknowingly startled a small animal and it ran away, rustling the tall grass.

Oblivious to the physical world around her, she strolled in the direction of the mountain where the sun set at the end of each day. The tall mountain was too far away to reach in an afternoon, but she could reach its foothills, where she wanted to climb just high enough to get a view of the whole village.

They had chosen their site carefully, midway between the foothills and the river. The ground where they built was flat enough for planting but high enough that if the river flooded, the village would be safe. A grove of fruit trees stood just upriver from the encampment, offering tasty apples and other fruits, as well as some relief from the cold wind that sometimes rushed through the river basin.

She remembered one of the Tribe's meetings to plan their village. Devin and the Hechtas talked all one night and into the next day, hashing out the best design and layout for the various buildings. They drew ideas in the dirt with a pointed stick, rubbing out a section that was rejected and drawing there again with another idea.

Long silences punctuated the meeting, a practice of the Hechtas. No Hechta was in the habit of thinking out loud, and they were comfortable enough together that their silences were not awkward.

This meeting had been extraordinary. They were not considering something simple, like when to begin summer travel or which route to take to the Summer Gathering. They were creating their home, and the difference between good choices and poor ones could have significant consequences. They all felt responsible to design a village that would bring joy and a sense of pride to everyone in the Tribe.

When an idea was presented or described, all listened, and

then considered it. When one woman had something to say, she said it. Often, there was more silence while the group considered her comments.

Garnet thought they had developed a good plan. They placed individual houses in a semi–circle with the openings downriver, facing away from the oncoming wind. A large, central area held the collective hearth, the children's house, the Elders' house, and Garnet's own. They planned a large, communal house near the hearth where they could gather when snow was deep or summer too hot.

Devin had told Garnet about a woman from a place called Solana she had met years ago at a Summer Gathering. What was her name? Garnet pondered a moment until it came to her. Ubakala? Yes, that was it. She and Devin were still friends after all this time. Ubakala told Devin how her desert people lived in a large house with walls made of hides. When the sun was too hot, they rolled up two of the hide walls to let a breeze blow through.

Devin had excitedly told Garnet about this design and her own modification to use layers of hides for walls in winter. She planned to fill spaces between the hides with grass and thatch to keep the warmth of the hearth fire inside.

Garnet smiled. Devin was always thinking about some new way to keep the Tribe warm, cool, fed, or happy. Garnet did not know if walls could hold the warmth in, but she had faith in her partner because Devin had a knack for useful ideas.

She even trained those dogs! Garnet shook her head, smiling at the creative thinking. Most Tribeswomen thought Devin had lost her mind when she first proposed the idea.

It began when two orphan dogs, still puppies really, followed Devin home from a hunt. Usually, the Tribe fed pups until they grew old enough to hunt on their own, when they were set free. But winter was coming on and Devin let the pups stay with her until spring. They even slept at her feet and kept them warm when Garnet could not.

Devin worked with the young dogs each day as they grew, teaching them to "stop" or "sit down" when she gave certain hand signals. Once spring came, the Elders asked when she planned to free the animals. Devin simply smiled and said that the dogs were free to leave any time they wished.

But it seemed these dogs wanted to stay. They romped with children each day, and Devin taught them to chase small objects that she tossed and return them to her. By late summer, she taught them to tolerate being harnessed to the spit and walk in a circle, turning the wheel that turned the roast.

One cool summer evening, a big feline lurked in the high grass near playing children. The closest dog growled a warning, and before the Hunters could react, both dogs barked furiously and chased the dangerous animal away. This quieted the Elders, who never again asked when the dogs would leave.

The dogs continued living with Devin and were adopted into the Tribe's life as if they had always been its companions. Garnet hoped her new garden would eventually become as well accepted.

She climbed the first grass–covered hills easily. As she went higher, the going became craggier and the muscles in her legs pulled and strained.

Her legs had felt this way once before, when she was ill and had to stay in bed several weeks. When she was able to walk on her own again, her leg muscles hurt for a while but eventually the pain subsided. Anna told her this was normal, that legs accustomed to walking every day became weak if unused for a time. She reassured Garnet that she would regain her leg–strength as she walked more and more.

It occurred to Garnet that if they lived in one place and did not travel far each season, the Tribeswomen might weaken from lack of movement, and she made a mental note to check with Anna about this.

As she reached the top of the third hill, she saw someone walking across the next slope, a man with a large walking stick. He stooped to pick something up and put it in a sack slung over his tall shoulder.

Suddenly, he seemed to sense her presence and he looked up, squinting, and saw her. She raised her hand in greeting; he raised his stick in return and walked her way.

Must be one of Falcone's people, a tall one, she thought. He was young, with dark, shaggy hair and the wiry build of one who walked long distances.

"Greetings, Mother!" he shouted as he came up the side of her hill.

"Toban?" She did not believe her eyes! Her heart leapt at the sight of her son, now grown into a man. This was once the chubby little boy she mothered? He was so. . . large!

As he approached, she saw him more clearly and recognized his grown–up features and his wide smile. They had not seen each other since he first went to live with the men when he was just 10 winters old. She reached to hug him and her arms had to extend as far as they could! He was a full head taller than she.

"Greetings, my son!" she smiled warmly, her arms still around his big shoulders. "What brings you so close to us?" The beard on his face scratched her skin.

"You look well!" He squeezed her tightly and grinned. "I have missed you!"

"And you have been busy growing tall and strong!" She beamed at him and reached up to rub his cheek as she had when he was small.

"Father said your people were near." He let go of her, suddenly self–conscious. "I was out to gather herbs and other items for the Healer, and I came this direction to look for your village. It is so large!"

"We intend to stay," she said, looking back over her shoulder at the distant camp, "so we need a lot of room."

"I remember you and Devin talking about building a place to live year–round. I do not think I would be happy in one place, but I wish you well." They stood a moment, looking at the village. "It is a good design. Devin planned well," Toban offered admiringly.

"She had a lot of help. Did your father say if he will visit?"

"Yes, when the moon rounds. He will send a messenger to Devin tomorrow to suggest it," Toban confided.

"I will enjoy visiting with you and your Tribesmen, and I want to show Falcone my garden." Stubborn Falcone would be hard to convince.

"You know Father does not believe that plants will grow where you bid. Of course, he believes in nothing that he cannot see or touch."

"Your father has been a good friend to me, Toban, but he does not know everything. He will see and believe when the harvest comes and he tastes bread made from grains we grew there," she said in a defensive tone.

Holding up his hands in surrender, he chuckled, "I believe you, Mama. I spent too many winters listening to your ideas to doubt you now, but Father is a stubborn man. I am not, since I am your son as well. I must return now with the herbs I have picked. They are needed."

"Is someone ill?"

"No, but Dain's joints pain him greatly, and Olen wants to make a salve that soothes them," Toban explained. "He is teaching me to make salves and powders. I wish to be a Healer one day if The Mother grants it."

"You will be a wonderful Healer, my son. I will not keep you from your duty, but it is so good to see you." She placed her hand on the young man's strong forearm and kissed his cheek, smiling.

"And you, beautiful one." He bowed and walked back the way he had come.

She watched him stride away, marveling at his growth. He was confident and well spoken, and she thought Falcone was doing a good job fathering the boy, which surprised her a little. She had always wondered if Falcone would be a good parent; he was so stubborn and set in his ways! But maybe all men were like that, she speculated. Garnet had not known many men in her lifetime, as they only visited once or twice a season, and some summers not at all.

She remembered the first time she and Falcone enjoyed each other's bodies. The men visited on a warm night of a round moon. There was wine and dancing, and Falcone was kind and strong. She enjoyed him, and they lay together again the following summer. First Toban, then Jori were born from these couplings. Garnet loved her children and had no regrets about the liaison with Falcone, though now she much preferred Devin's company to that of any man.

Over many seasons, Falcone had proven to be a good friend and now it seemed he was a good father as well. She looked forward to catching up on stories and sharing a meal with him and his Tribesmen.

Some women no doubt wanted to share the pleasures of men and would perhaps become pregnant. The youngest child in the village had been born two winters ago.

Garnet knew that union with a man caused pregnancy, but she did not know why sometimes such unions produced a child and other times they did not. Some seasons the village had three or four babies, and other times, none. It was another of The Mother's mysteries, she supposed, like, why some women enjoyed pleasures with men, others with women, and some with both. No one knew why, it just was.

Garnet could no longer see Toban in the distance, so she turned to view her village again. Scanning the vista slowly, she smiled and thought, it is a fine place, and we have plenty of room to grow.

She sat in fragrant grass and contemplated the land and sky before her, enjoying all that she saw and the warmth of the sun caressing her skin. Something about the combination of the smell of grass and her skin's warm tingle from the sun made Garnet relax. She leaned on one elbow, raising her face to the sky and shaking her head to loosen her full, red mane.

She felt wonderful and frightened at the same time to see her dreams begin to manifest. This change was such a radical departure from how her Tribe had always lived! She felt the culture and ways of the Tribe resting on her shoulders, and they suddenly tightened. Calm down, she told herself firmly. Do not let negative thoughts take over.

She breathed deeply to clear her heart. She could not show doubt now, as her unshakable belief was what had convinced the Tribeswomen to try her plan in the first place. And as she thought the situation through, she realized that if her plan failed, the worst that might happen was that the Tribe would have to return to traveling.

As for their more immediate needs, Devin and the Hunters were making sure that they would have plenty of food for the winter in case their garden failed.

She assured herself that her Tribeswomen's health and safety were at very little risk. They were near a good water source and a bountiful orchard. They would all be fine, she nodded decisively, feeling peace return to her outlook. The Tribe was whole and healthy, and the plants in the garden grew well. They would be fine in the coming winter.

When the sun was high in the sky the next day, Devin's Scouts came running into the village to report that a messenger from the men's Tribe approached from the mountains.

Devin climbed down from the roof she was thatching and

summoned Barde to announce the arrival. She sent Jori, who helped again today, to tell Garnet and then the Hechtas. Devin thought the Hechtas probably knew of the visitor already, but custom and courtesy required their notification.

"Mother! Mother! They are coming!" Jori shouted, running to Garnet's house.

Smiling, Garnet came out the door as the child arrived.

"Who comes, dear one?" she asked, though she thought she knew.

"A messenger!" Jori pranced excitedly. "They told Devin they would visit once they were settled, and it looks like they will! Devin says to come to the hearth and greet the messenger. Barde sings the Visitor Song, and Devin told me to tell the Hechtas, too!"

Garnet's eyes sparkled at her daughter's excitement. "That is an important assignment, and I will not keep you. I will go to the hearth shortly."

The child sprinted toward the trees. Only when she approached the Hechtas' home did she slow to a more dignified pace, knowing it was not wise to raise dust in the faces of these women.

Nita sat on a stump in front of the house, grinding an herb into powder with a stone. "Good morning, young Hunter," she smiled heartily at the child. "What brings you here?"

"Devin sent me to tell you that a messenger from the men's Tribe comes. She asks everyone to meet at the hearth to greet him," the child recited dutifully.

"Thank you, Jori," Nita's velvety voice replied solemnly. "We are aware of his approach, and we prepare to greet the messenger. Tell Devin we will arrive soon."

Women talked with excitement as they gathered around the

central hearth area. The Hechtas arrived and stood near Garnet, nodding their greeting to Devin.

The runner entered the village, and Devin stepped forward to greet him, smiling when she saw it was her old friend, Lexis. He looked fit and returned her smile with his own wide grin. She grasped his hands, then stepped back and composed her face to offer the formal words of greeting.

"Greetings, brother," she said loudly. "You are welcome in our home, Lexis."

"Greetings, sister," he smiled at her, bowing formally. "I come with a message from Falcone. Our Tribe wishes to visit your people at the next moon's round. We will bring our drums and pipes, and we wish to make music and merriment and share news."

"Thank you for the message, my brother," Devin returned his bow and gestured to the long tables nearby. "Will you eat and rest yourself a time? I will soon have a response for Falcone."

Lexis bowed again. "Thank you, sister. You are most kind." He walked to the table and sat, smiling. Several women served him food and drink or just came to sit and chat.

Devin turned to the assembled Tribeswomen and asked, "What say you to this messenger? Do you wish a visit on the next round?"

All the women agreed. Devin scanned the eager faces and saw that even Shayana smiled.

"Good. I will tell Falcone that we welcome his Tribe."

The Queens and the Hechtas took seats around one table and shared a meal with the resting runner. The Tribe was generous and treated its guests with great courtesy. Other women crowded to sit at tables nearby.

Nita pulled a pouch from her robe and handed it to Lexis. "I understand that one of your old ones suffers from stiffness.

Please give this powder to your Healer for a tea. After such a long winter, he cannot have much medicine on hand."

"This is true, sister," Lexis said, inclining his head to her. "Thank you for your kindness. It has been a long winter. The snows followed us almost all the way to the sea."

"Do you need grain or fruit?" Garnet asked, concerned. "We can share some if you like."

Lexis shook his head, smiling appreciatively, "No, but thank you. We are fine."

"Please tell Falcone that we gladly accept his offer of a visit. We will prepare a feast in your honor on the next round moon, for the time of day when the sun sets," Devin spoke the formal phrases. "We look forward to seeing our friends."

"Your friends look forward to seeing you!" The man smiled wryly, inclining his head again.

Devin returned his impish grin. She liked this man with green eyes that twinkled when he smiled. They first became friends when they were children, and the bond remained. She looked down the table and saw merry twinkles in many eyes. Marjika in particular smiled warmly at Lexis, and he glanced at her frequently.

"Did you see him? Why do they bow like that?" Jori bowed down and back up three times in quick succession.

The girls hid nearby behind bales of grass. Children were not part of the welcoming ceremony, but they always managed to find a safe spot to hide and watch.

Ara giggled, "You look like those sea birds that dunk their heads in waves for fish to eat!"

"Shh! They will hear and chase us away," Jori cautioned.

"Why are men so hairy?" Ara whispered loudly. "They look like little Bears."

"Maybe the fur keeps them warm!" Kelan offered.

"There is not enough for that," Riala countered. "It is not like they have real fur all over. That would be nicer. Theirs just grows in patches."

"I do not know. I think they stink, though." Jori made a face. "I can smell him from here."

"Maybe it is the toads," Ara mused.

"Toads?" Jena was alarmed at the thought. "What toads?"

"Mother said their Tribe considers the Toad a messenger of The Mother. Maybe they carry their sacred Toads around with them, and that is why they stink!" Jori suggested, having great fun at her sister's expense.

"They do not stink!" Kelan exploded.

"They will bathe before they visit," Jena offered wisely, "because they want women to like them, to dance and talk and make pleasure."

"Ewww!" Jori's face contorted in disgust. "I will never get that close to them! I would like to see Toban, though," she added thoughtfully. "Devin says he has grown tall and brown. Maybe he will play catch–the–ball with us."

"That will be fun!" Ara remembered enjoying time with Toban.

"He is not interested in children's games," Riala tossed her head haughtily in a gesture reminiscent of Kelan. "He is grown now. Maybe he wants to dance with me . . ."

"Humph," Jori huffed. "Devin said only that he has grown taller, NOT that he has lost his wits."

"You are such a child!" Kelan snapped. "You do not understand anything! When boys grow to men, they change. They think of women differently from how they did when they were little."

"Then I do not care if he comes here at all! I have seen women dancing and talking and sneaking off with them. Frankly, I would rather go hunting!" Jori stalked away, followed by Ara, dismissing the whole visit.

Murmuring voices blended with shuffling feet to form a quiet river of sound as members of the Tribe filed around the hearth fire and sat in a large circle. Garnet had asked everyone to assemble but had not told them why, and all awaited the Queens' arrival.

With no information as to the reason for this last–minute meeting, women worried aloud; speculation abounded.

"Do you think something is wrong with the planting?" one asked.

"Perhaps Lexis brought news that he shared only with Garnet," another suggested.

"Is someone ill?" one worried, bringing gasps and comments of, "I hope not!"

A curtain of silence descended as Garnet and Devin joined the group, and Garnet got right to the point. "We must decide what to do about the Summer Gathering. The men will visit on the night of the moon when we usually have a Council meeting, so I have asked you to assemble now instead to decide on Gathering plans." She knew her people well.

Her sentence ended to a collective, "Oooh!" She gave the women a moment to settle and share their anticipation and relief.

"What is there to decide?" Tem refocused them. "We always attend the Gathering. One of our Tribe serves in the Consistory, and I will be sad if I do not see Norahjen this summer."

Gatherings of the Sisters occurred each summer at a site that sat at the edge of the sea, many days' walk downriver. Tribes from far–away places trekked to the shore to share knowledge and stories, compare beliefs and experiences, and to celebrate. They traded goods and news; they sang, danced, ate, laughed, and loved. But most of all, they reminded themselves that all women come from The Mother no matter what their differences.

Comprised of Elders from various tribes, a group called the Consistory organized and planned the Gathering. Their job began in mid–spring, with helpers joining as the Gathering time drew closer.

The Consistory Elders directed a huge array of activities, everything that was needed to create a temporary village for many women. Women gathered fuel for fires, built fire circles, and cleared the large dance ground of flotsam and shells from the sea. Some gathered and preserved food for the Gathering's feasts; some hunted herbs and other medicines. By the end of spring, the number of women at the Gathering site grew from just five Elders to a group as numerous as Garnet's Tribe.

Some women joined the Consistory or acted as helpers for just one season; some continued their service over many years, considering it their life's work to serve The Mother this way. Each woman's sacred choice was encouraged and accepted. It was an honor for a Tribeswoman to serve on the Consistory, and service to one another was at the heart of the Gathering's spirit.

Norahjen had been in the Consistory for the past several Gatherings. In winter she returned to her Tribe and worked with Astaga and Herta. She was a Hechta and an Elder. She had been a Scout in her younger days, but she long ago turned those duties over to her apprentice, saying she was now "too old to run and too big to hide." Tem smiled, thinking of her friend's strong, lined face. No matter how serious her expression, Norahjen's green eyes always twinkled with mirth.

What a contrast between the ranting bitterness of Shayana and the calm, wise guidance of Norahjen, she thought. Age is a funny thing. For some, old age was a time of regret and physical ailments; for others like Norahjen, it was a time of ripening and wisdom. Tem wondered why the difference.

Norahjen had always been a strong and calming figure in the Tribe. Tem remembered the first summer she hunted when she fell down a cliff and broke her foot. Norahjen was the one who found her and carried her back to camp.

Tem was lucky the bones healed well. She remembered the terrible pain and the one little bone sticking through the skin on top of her foot. But what she remembered most was the feeling of safety that washed over her when the big Scout picked her up.

She was shaken out of her reverie by the questioning voice of the Hearth Queen. "Tem?"

"Oh, um, I am sorry, what?" Tem answered, embarrassed to be caught daydreaming.

"I am not saying that we should or should not go, dear," Garnet explained, "but since we have settled here, we have to plan for the trip. Each woman will decide for herself what to do."

"Well, I wish to go even if no one else does," Tem grumbled staunchly.

"It is important for each woman to decide for herself," Barde said. "Each woman has that right, and no one wants to take that away."

"Yes, I agree," Daña said, looking at Tem. "I have no desire to go, but I do not object to others going. Every woman makes her own choice."

"It is so," Garnet agreed. "Again, let me say I do not propose to decide for anyone, but if some want to go, we need to begin planning."

"When do we have to leave, Devin?" Barde asked the Hunt Queen.

"In order to arrive at the Gathering by the round moon after Lammas, we have to leave on the new moon before," Devin spoke slowly, staring thoughtfully into the flames. "We will return a few days after the following crescent."

"Why do we have to go at all?" Shayana's strident voice cut through the night. "We have so much work to do here, now that you have all decided to stay in this place."

"For the reasons we always go to the Gathering, Shayana — to see other Tribes, to trade, and to learn from them," Anna said in a calm voice as she scooted closer to the old woman, sensing an imminent episode.

"We have nothing to learn from anyone!" Shayana was excited and the pitch of her voice rose to an uncomfortable level for most women's ears. "Our Tribe has survived countless generations just as we are! I object to all these upsetting practices! Norahjen is a fool! Her duty is to stay with us, not run off to plan a big feast!"

Ahh, thought Garnet, the old one is jealous. In their youth, Shayana had wanted Norahjen as a romantic partner, but Norahjen was not interested. Maybe Norahjen spends her summers elsewhere to avoid the bitter Shayana, Garnet thought wryly.

"All of you talk about change as if it is always a GOOD thing!" She cackled on, "You endanger us with that kind of talk!" The agitated woman rocked and talked faster, flailing her fist through the air. "Dogs that cook! Plants that grow where you want them! Next you will ask a herd of elk to build a village next to us and lie down so that you can kill them without going on a hunt. It is unnatural!"

Lia moved closer to help Anna calm Shayana, who eventually quieted but continued to mumble incoherently. On her other side, Anna whispered comforting words.

"Shayana's point of view has merit," Alecia the Elder said quietly. She had supported Garnet's idea to stay here and plant a garden, albeit reluctantly.

"Oh, not the ranting, mind you. But if we are to survive a winter without traveling as we always have, we have a lot of work to do. I am willing to try Garnet's plan even though I have doubts, but we must do the work to ensure our survival whether her plan works or not. Some of you seem to forget that. Why, when I was a girl . . ."

"But Alecia," Daña interjected, "I was at the garden the other day and I saw for myself. Seeds that Garnet planted sprout every day, and much of the growing will continue until well after everyone returns from the Gathering. We have plenty of time to prepare for winter."

"I agree with Daña," said Wren. "There is time enough both to do the work and for those women who want to travel to attend the Gathering. Everyone does not wish to make the trip; some will stay here, in our home."

A cheer rose from the Tribe and Garnet's eyes brimmed. The women did believe in their new home! She felt the warm pressure of Devin's hand squeezing hers. Devin knew the importance of this moment as well.

"Whoever stays here has to look after the garden," Garnet said, wiping her eyes. They have to look after Shayana, too, she thought to herself sarcastically, but Anna chuckled as though she had said it out loud. Garnet saw the mirth in Anna's eyes and grinned at the Healer.

"I will see to the garden," Daña offered.

"I will help," said Lia.

"So, we agree that each will decide for herself for her own reasons whether or not she goes to the Gathering. I will organize preparations and guide the travelers," Devin announced.

"I suggest we all take a little time to think this over. There is no hurry," Garnet said softly, using her beautiful voice to calm the group. "Let Devin know if you wish to go by midsummer so that she may prepare thoughtfully."

"Remember, too," Devin chimed in, "if you go to the Gathering, you also need to decide on the work you will contribute. I need to know who will teach a lesson, who will help with children, who will help prepare food. You know all of the jobs to be done, and if you do not, come and talk with me. Some of us may leave a little earlier than others depending on the jobs we choose. As soon as I know your choices, I will send a runner to inform the Consistory so they can include us in their plans."

SPRING
1984 C.E.

"At least I have a shovel now," she said, laughing at my exertion. "I once had only a flat stick."

I muttered an oath, turning another clump of earth over and chopping at it with the shovel's end. My feet hurt even through boots, and the seeping blisters on my hands burned. We had been at this since sunrise. Well, I had been at it. As usual, she only supervised. Even in the chill of an early spring morning, sweat dripped from me.

"You have almost finished this part," she said.

"This part? There's another part?" I stopped mid–chop and looked at her with consternation and fatigue.

"Of course. This area is just for seeds we plant every year."

"What's the other part?" I asked wearily.

"The dirt around the perennials must be loosened and fed," she said in a tone that emphasized my ignorance.

I heaved a great sigh and returned to chopping. Who did this physical labor for her last spring, I wondered. I didn't ask out loud; I knew she would simply grimace and say, "I did."

The old woman offered to make lunch while I finished this

section, and she hobbled back to the house. I could not imagine her frail little body doing this heavy work.

How long had she lived here alone, I wondered. She told me she lived here with others until the rest died. She took me to the place where she held their funeral fires, and I still have a handful of the soil from there in a little glass jar. It sits on a shelf near the pouch of seeds she gave me on my last day with her. Every now and then, I pick up the little jar and peer inside, wondering which of my ancestors might be in there.

I could not find a link between the chores she kept assigning me and the lessons she claimed to want to teach me. So far, she had only revealed a few stories at night as we sat in front of the fireplace.

I had expected great pontifications, wondrous magical lessons. What I got was a crafty, ancient wood sprite with a wry sense of humor who expected me to work without complaint all day and listen quietly as she rambled into the night.

I cannot say that her stories were not interesting, but I continued to feel that she wasn't any more ready to trust me with all her information than I was to trust her. And so I worked and waited for the real lessons to begin.

In retrospect, I can see that those early talks had some of the biggest lessons of all, but at the time, I didn't understand. I asked many questions and got many cynical looks in return. She rarely answered a question directly. More often, she simply glared until I was quiet and then continued with her story.

Sometimes to this very day when I try to tell my rebellious adolescent children a story, I catch a memory of her looking at me like that, and I smile.

Summer
3783 B.C.E.

"Why do we pull some plants from the dirt?" Kelan whined. Black soil caked her hands, and she held them stiffly away from her body, disgustedly trying to shake off the dirt. "You promised us a swim!"

Kelan's incessant complaining could be more irritating than the little stinging mosquitoes, Garnet thought. "After your chores are done, we will go to the river," her voice remained serene. "We must all do our part so everyone can eat. Make sure you get the roots, too."

"Why is that important, Mother?" Jori chimed in with a much lighter tone. She was covered with silty loam from head to foot but she barely seemed to notice. Wiping her brow with a filthy hand, she left a streak of black mud across her forehead.

"If you just pull the top of the plant without also getting the roots, the same plant will just grow there again. If we want these plants gone for good, we must pull out everything, roots and all," Garnet explained.

The children pulled strays out of the garden, not the plants that they had planted seeds for themselves. Garnet explained that these strays took nourishment and filled up the space that the food plants needed.

All the children helped, even little Marianna. Garnet assigned Kelan to stay close to the youngest one, lest she pull out as many food plants as she did strays.

Marjika and Anna sat near the patch of turned earth, sorting through the strays the children piled there. Anna used many of these to concoct healing teas, salves, and potions. Marjika set aside the ones useful in 'majikal' potions for Nita. The Tribe rarely wasted anything, as they believed it dishonored The Mother's gifts if they did not use and enjoy all that they could.

"The garden comes along nicely," Daña commented as she walked up.

"Yes," Garnet replied, standing and assessing their progress. "We must keep out these stray plants, though, and it is a good job for the children. Your little one even helps."

"She so loves being with the older ones," Daña smiled indulgently at the black mop of tangles bouncing toward her, "and it is good for her to help."

"I promised them a swim when we finish. I will take Marianna along, too, if you allow," Garnet said hopefully. She enjoyed the little girl's bubbly presence.

"She will love that!" Ignoring copious amounts of mud that adorned the child, Daña hefted her up into the air and the two laughed together at the thrill. "She can keep her head above water, and I trust Kelan to watch out for her."

"Are you done with the central house already?" Anna sounded surprised. Daña and Devin had worked on the large building for several days.

"Yes, we just now finished, with a lot of help," Daña grinned proudly.

The women's custom held that she who was to live in a house always helped build it, and since this house was for the entire Tribe, almost everyone wanted to lend a hand. Devin and

Daña stayed busy teaching and supervising women who did not normally build shelters, but they managed the project with good humor, grateful for the extra hands that sped the work. All sang happy songs, mindful to infuse a joyful spirit into the structure.

One of the Tribe's basic beliefs was that all actions and the intent behind them are important. The builders believed that their intent was as important as their skills when they created something. To build a house with joy in one's heart brought joy to the house; to cook food with a healthy intent brought good health to those who ate it. "As within, so without," the Hechtas said, meaning that the intent in one's heart and mind naturally manifested in her creations in the physical world. Judging from the joyful faces of the women who built it, this house would bring the Tribe great happiness.

From the time they could first hear and understand, this Tribe's children were taught to clear their minds and establish their intent before starting any task. One might feel worry or anger for a short time, and when these powerful emotions arose they had to be acknowledged, expressed, and released, sometimes in private, sometimes with others. A woman was then free to continue her original activity with a clean heart.

Sometimes women had difficulty letting go of worry, resentment, or fear. When this happened, she might go to the Healers or the Hechtas for counsel. Sometimes a long walk near water helped; sometimes just talking until the feelings weakened did the trick. Occasionally, she required a ritual or an herbal solution to help clear her heart and mind.

If a woman had a problem that did not let her go, she could stay in the Temple for a time, which the Tribe called "dark time." Whatever her level of discontent or malaise, the woman received the care she needed from her Tribemates. Each woman was an important part of the whole, so the Tribe valued and cared for every member, and each had equal access to healing resources.

At first Jori was upset this morning when her mother did not let her help finish building the house. She ranted and stormed, hoping to get her way, but Garnet took her on a short walk to the river. They skipped flat stones over the water and chatted about the garden and its importance to the Tribe. Soon, Jori felt happier, and they went to the task.

"Can you all come and see the new house? Devin sent me to ask," Daña looked hopefully at Garnet.

"Certainly! This is a big occasion," she said to Daña as she turned to the children, who all looked expectantly at the two adults. "Well, come on then!" Their cheering drowned her next sentence, "But only for a little while, then back to work."

The children ran toward the village center with Jori in the lead as usual.

Marjika's pregnancy was just beginning to show. As Anna helped her to her feet, she remembered the joyful visit of the men's tribe that had led up to it. Daña swung little Marianna up to her shoulders and followed in step with Garnet.

"Are you well, Marjika?" Garnet asked as they strolled along.

"I am much happier now that I am no longer sick every morning." Marjika walked stiffly, holding her hands on her belly as though it might fall off if she let go. "I am adjusting to the difference in my balance. I am not yet used to being so much heavier in the middle."

Garnet smiled, knowing the pregnancy was not really that far along yet but indulging Marjika's concerns.

"You are fine, dear," Anna assured the young woman. This was Marjika's first child, and she was more worried than the experienced mothers. The Healers made a concerted effort to keep the young woman calm and confidant.

In all, three Tribeswomen became pregnant this spring during the visit by Falcone's Tribe. Healers visited each one regularly to be sure that they were well, and so far, all three mothers–to–be progressed as healthy mothers should.

The women walked past the circle of houses at the edge of the village and saw what looked like the entire Tribe gathered around the new building, all pointing and talking excitedly.

The Tribeswomen made way for Garnet, many appearing to suppress smiles, and Garnet's curiosity was aroused when she saw Devin at the building entrance. Arms crossed over her chest, Devin had a stubborn look that meant someone annoyed her. Nearby, Shayana glowered angrily. Seeing Garnet approach, Devin lightened considerably.

"It is fitting for the Hearth Queen to see this first, my love," she said, bowing to Garnet, then kissing her cheek.

"It is fitting for the eldest to enter first!" snapped Shayana.

The crowd groaned. Most of the women indulged Shayana as she was, after all, the longest–living woman in two generations, but a few resented her contrary outbursts.

"You are not the Hearth Queen, Shayana. You will see the building soon enough," Devin tried to control her tone.

With a deep breath, Garnet assessed the situation and had an idea.

She winked at Devin, then spoke to Shayana, "Please come in with me, dear," Garnet said sweetly to the disturbed woman.

Garnet thought it was no surprise that Shayana had lived so long. She rarely took any risks, preferring to keep everything in her life exactly as it always had been. Besides, Garnet thought, she was just too stubborn to die. Smiling indulgently, she gestured for Shayana to precede her. "Let us see it together."

Shayana hobbled in front of Garnet and looked triumphantly at Devin. Garnet smiled warmly while Devin rolled her eyes and sighed. Garnet squeezed her partner's hand reassuringly, and, with a nod for Daña to join them, entered the building.

Garnet stopped just inside the door to take it all in. Mouth agape, she looked all around at the large building. A huge central area had four rooms going off in four directions. A round, low stone wall at the very center of the center had flat stones along the top about as high as Garnet's waist. On one side of the stone wall was an opening. Earth had been dug out so that the area inside the stone wall was lower than the rest of the floor. Garnet saw a hole above the small stone circle. She turned to Devin, puzzled. "A hearth?"

Devin beamed. "Exactly! To keep us warm and to cook food and heat water when snows are deep. We put one in the meat storage house, too," she chattered quickly like an excited child. "See these two notches in the wall? They will hold each end of a spit. There is not enough room for the turning wheel or the dogs in here, but we do not usually have big feasts when snows are high anyway. Now we can; we just have to turn the spit ourselves."

"This whole building will burn down the first time you light a fire in here!" Shayana interrupted in her shrill voice. "What are you girls thinking?" she howled, storming from the building.

Daña giggled. "She can move quickly when she is angry!"

"She will be sore later from the exertion," Garnet worried aloud. "All that stomping is hard on her old knees."

"I predict she will be happy enough to sleep near this fire when winter snows pile high!" Devin quipped, then whispered to Garnet, "And you still should have walked in first!"

"Thank you for your consideration, darling," Garnet gently laid her hand on Devin's well–muscled arm. "I merely placated Shayana to quiet her. It is my job to keep peace inside the village, you know."

"I suppose," Devin's deep voice rumbled and she looked rather like a recalcitrant child.

Garnet walked around the hearth and peered in each room. The two rooms to the East and West were the same size, but the room to the South was much larger and longer than the one at the North. Garnet guessed why but she asked anyway, knowing that Devin would enjoy the telling.

"The rooms represent the seasons of the sun. This one," Devin gestured to the smallest, "points in the direction of the ice lands and is smallest. It honors the winter Solstice, when days are shortest. These," she gestured toward the East and West rooms, "are for the Equinoxes in spring and fall, when day and night are the same. And this one," gesturing to the South, "is for midsummer, when days are longest. The circle hearth at the center represents our Tribe's home."

Women who had crowded into the doorway murmured their approval, and Devin suddenly noticed her audience. Tears welled over many eyes, including Garnet's.

"I am so proud. This is magnificent and beautiful, like the women who built it," Garnet announced.

They stood in silence, admiring the magnificent, sturdy building. Garnet's hand rested gently on her mate's shoulder.

"The ledges are for storage, I suppose, or sitting," Garnet guessed, pointing along the walls of the winter room.

"In case we are snowed–in, we can put our food up off the ground on these ledges," Daña said, as excited as Devin. Their passion was contagious.

"Let us hope that snows never get THAT high!" Garnet wished.

After she made a complete circle around the hearth, Garnet hugged Devin and Daña. "It is amazing!" she grinned at them both. "Thank you so much for all of your hard and smart work."

"We plan to hang hides along all the walls to keep warmth

in during cold times," Daña explained enthusiastically. "Devin learned that from a desert Tribe."

"A desert Tribe?" Astaga asked, puzzled. "They live in tents, do they not? And is it not always hot where they live? Why would they build anything that will keep us warm?"

"During rainy seasons it gets cold at night in the desert. They showed me how they weave camel hair and sheep's wool into big, flat hides that they call 'rugs.' They hang these rugs on walls inside their tents and they cover the ground with them. They say these rugs keep heat out on hot days and keep heat in during cold nights. We decided that hides will work the same way."

"You are amazing! You take everything you learn from our friends at Gathering and use it to help us," Garnet beamed at the women.

"I want to trade the men for some sheep's wool when it grows long and try to make a rug next winter, too," Daña told her.

Women left the building so the children could come in and see. Garnet smiled at everyone and shared her delight. "You have all done a fine job! The builders told me that nearly every woman in the Tribe helped. This wonderful house will shelter us all."

Garnet waited for the children to tour all over, then took them back to the garden. They finished weeding without much grumbling, so she took them to swim.

"Do you ever go near the river without an adult?" Garnet asked the littlest child as she carried her to the river bank.

"Oh, no!" Marianna replied. "Mama tolded me. Only when someone is with me."

"There is a good girl," Garnet smiled at her. "This will be fun, eh?"

No sooner had the child's feet touched the ground than she ran off, chasing Kelan into the water.

Jori and Ara had run ahead and were already downstream. From the grassy bank, Garnet saw them bending to the river's surface, looking under the water.

"Look, Mother, I got a fish!" Jori yelled excitedly, pointing to the bank where Garnet saw a large, wriggling fish.

Ara tried but all she managed to scoop up was a lot of water. Garnet smiled, thinking she would get the knack eventually.

"Good job!" Garnet shouted. "But, Jori, this is time to play, not to fish. Do not kill creatures needlessly." She tossed the slippery fish back into the river.

Actually, a fish dinner sounds good, she thought, and decided to ask Devin to lead a fishing trip soon. Many Hunters fished with only their hands, as the Great Bear had taught them years before. Garnet remembered the lesson well.

She and Devin had been on a learning trip with the Scouts in these very foothills. Garnet thought she must have been quite small at the time because in her memory, Norahjen seemed a giant.

The day was hot and the Tribe was resting. When they thought everyone else was asleep, Devin and Garnet crept to the river, practicing their stealth. As they snuck through the brush on the river bank, they heard an unmistakable sound and froze on the spot. A large Mother Bear and Her cubs waded in the water just a few feet away.

Garnet remembered as if it were yesterday the chill of fear that ran up her back when she saw the Bears and the absolute relief that washed over her when she felt Norahjen's big hand on her back, cautioning her to stay quiet.

The Bear looked at the humans for a long moment, then returned to fishing as though they were not there. They watched Her stand still looking at the river, then scoop a fish quickly from the water with Her powerful paws.

Around that evening's campfire, after giving them a good scolding for wandering off without an adult, Norahjen told the girls that the Bear had given them a great gift by letting them watch Her.

Devin spent the entire summer practicing the Bear's fishing method, determined not to squander the gift. She became so good that most of the other Hunters wanted to learn, too. Many picked up the skill quickly, and those who did not still used their spears to catch fish the older, more familiar way. These many seasons later, Garnet watched her daughter as she practiced. Jori took to the Bear's way of fishing as if she were a little cub herself.

Garnet walked upstream toward Kelan, who was teaching the littlest one to float. Kelan cradled Marianna as she lay on her back atop the water and helped her move gently through the stream. The child kicked her feet and giggled with delight. Little droplets of water landed on Kelan's arms, raising bumps from the chill. Garnet waded out to the girls.

"You must lie still if you want to float, dear," Kelan spoke gently to the baby. "Only kick your feet when you want to swim."

Garnet smiled approvingly at Kelan and rested her hand on the girl's shoulder. "You teach her well, my daughter. Your patience is impressive and you have a gentle way with children. It shows your kindness of heart."

Kelan's eyes glistened at the compliment. She was only doing what came naturally to her, and Mama praised her! She looked to see if her friends had heard, and when she saw that they had, her chest swelled.

She did love small children. Whenever she had time to herself, she went to the little ones' house and helped Grandmothers care for them. There had been no babies last season, she knew, but next season, there might be three! Perhaps she could attend the births.

She looked up hopefully. "There will be more babies this year, Mother."

"Yes, three women are pregnant now," Garnet agreed.

"May I go with you to the births?" she held her breath waiting as she rocked the toddler in shallow water.

Garnet looked into the eager little eyes. "You may," she assented. "It can sometimes take a long time, though, and always, there is blood." Garnet did not want Kelan to faint at a birthing.

"I know, Mother," she said quickly.

"All right, then."

Riala and Jena gasped. To be allowed to attend a birth! Kelan was so lucky! Giggling, they swam off to tell Jori and Ara.

Kelan took this opportunity to tell her mother something important. Taking a deep breath, she began, "Mother, I want you to know, when Jori killed that buck on the hunt, it was not the blood that bothered me," Kelan explained.

"What, then?" Garnet was glad for a chance to ask. She had waited for the child to bring up this subject when she was ready.

"It was the suddenness of the buck's death. It was so quick! The buck stood there enjoying his day, and then he was dead. I felt a sudden emptiness where the buck had been," she paused thoughtfully. "I felt pulled toward it, like the underwater currents you warn us about in the river. When I tried to resist the pull, I got all dizzy."

Garnet jolted with excitement. Did this child actually feel the creature's spirit depart? Her training had not even begun! Taking a deep breath to keep her voice calm, she asked, "Did you see the buck fall?"

"I do not remember," the girl looked at the sky to search her memory. "Everything became foggy for a moment, then the fog thinned. Next thing I remember, I was sitting on the grass with Tem talking to me."

"I see," Garnet said thoughtfully. She must tell the Hechtas of this!

Loud laughter made Garnet look downstream, where she saw Riala sitting in the water, looking angry while the others laughed. Garnet went to see what the matter was.

"Riala? Are you all right, dear?"

"I am quite all right," Riala stood, rubbing her behind.

"She is fine, Mother," Jori chuckled, "but if she had to fish or starve, she would surely starve!"

"And have a sore bottom, too!" Ara laughed.

Even Jena smiled, though she tried not to laugh at her friend's expense.

"Now, Jori," Garnet admonished her daughter, "there are many things Riala excels in that you cannot do well. It is not polite to laugh when someone tries to learn a new skill."

"Yes, Mother," Jori lowered her head with false humility, knowing that she could tease Riala later!

Garnet let the children play for a time and then coaxed them to the bank. They walked upriver, then turned inland toward home. All along their path, children looked with great interest at fallen trees, patches of grass, and stones in the path. They dutifully brought found treasures to Garnet for explanation or permission to keep. With the toddler slung over her shoulder, Kelan walked along easily beside Garnet, chatting happily.

Several mornings later, just as the sun rose, Jori and Ara laid face down in high grass that bordered the garden. Jori's chest and belly were wet with dew, and she could smell the sweet odor of the stalks her body had just crushed. As a stray feathery stalk tickled her neck, she decided it was well worth the discomfort to keep quiet.

They had received permission to hunt rabbits that were eating the succulent greens in the garden. Garnet let them cajole her for a while before consenting. The girls argued that once rabbits knew they would be hunted in a certain place, they would stop coming there. By hunting the rabbits, they reasoned, they were helping chase them from the garden permanently.

Garnet replied that making noise and scaring the rabbits away achieved the same end. While true, the girls conceded, Garnet's approach did not also provide rabbit stew or pelts for the Tribe. Garnet finally consented but she told them to get Devin's permission as well.

Devin offered Jori and Ara helpful suggestions, showing them how to mask their human scent by rubbing the smelly sap of a particular plant on their skin. She instructed them to lie very still in the tall grass, upwind of the garden. Tall stalks waving in the wind hid accidental movements the young hunters made. Finally, she took them to Astaga, the Toolmaker.

Astaga checked their bows for cracks, the strings for wear, and the arrows for sharpness. She presented each girl with a long hide pouch in which to carry her arrows. The pouch had a strap so it could be hung over the shoulder, and Astaga called it a "quiver."

Now Jori laid by the garden, the smell of damp earth in her nostrils. She was glad for Ara's steady breathing nearby. Jori's bow was on the ground in front of her, an arrow notched and ready. She turned her head slightly to look at Ara, who was ready as well and returned her excited smile.

They must stay perfectly silent and still now. Jori blinked as a bug crawled onto her face. She blew at it hard, trying to dislodge it. The bug continued its crawl toward her eyes until she finally flicked it off with her finger.

The sun was rising, and its low angle made both girls squint. Jori tilted her face slowly, using the thick blades of grass to shield her eyes from the glare.

She was about to move her hand up to her eyes when she sensed movement beside the garden. She froze. There! She saw it again! A rabbit! It advanced a few steps closer and stopped, head up, sniffing the air, and looking nervous.

The rabbit came a few cautious steps more. Its little nose twitched nonstop, and Jori's every muscle tensed in excitement. She willed herself to relax, took a deep breath, and wondered: What would Devin do?

This first rabbit would be followed by others if they saw that it found no danger, and the girls knew they had a better chance for a kill after more rabbits came in range.

They waited on edge for what seemed like hours, and finally two more rabbits approached the garden's edge. Feeling quite safe now, the poachers munched happily on succulent shoots as three more arrived and began breakfast.

Jori slowly reached for her bow. The silence was so complete that all she could hear was the sound of rabbits chewing. And then . . .

"WHY ARE YOU TRYING TO EAT THAT GRASS?" Riala's strident voice shrieked behind them.

The rabbits scattered.

"Look, Kelan!" Riala shouted. "They are rubbing themselves in mud!"

Jori sprang to her feet, furious. She tackled Riala and they tumbled to the ground, arms flailing. "You . . . you . . . we were hunting rabbits in the garden!"

"You scared them all away!" Ara jumped up and yelled, her face bright red with anger.

Kelan and Jena arrived to pull Jori off Riala. Jori kicked and punched at them all.

"Leave Riala alone!" Kelan demanded as she and Jena held a struggling Jori tightly.

"SHE should have left US alone! We were hunting!" Jori shouted.

"You were not going to kill anything, anyway," Jena taunted.

"How do you know?" snapped Jori, pushing off Jena's hands. "You do not even HAVE a bow."

"Oh, come on, Jori. It is not like a rabbit is going to walk right up and stand still so you can kill it," Kelan said, letting go of her sister.

"WHAT?" Jori yelled in shock, then lunged for Kelan, truly angry at her sister's unfair sarcasm about her first kill. Jena and Riala went after Jori, and the entire pile tumbled to the ground again.

"At least she would not faint if it did!" Ara shot back, jumping onto Kelan's back.

Alerted by the noise, Daña waded into the fray.

"You girls calm down!" she ordered, separating them all. "What is this about?"

The girls all began talking loudly at once. Daña held up her hand and shouted, "ENOUGH!" until the girls quieted. "Come with me. We will ask the Hearth Queen to settle this."

Daña walked resolutely toward Garnet's house with the girls marching sullenly behind. Upon their arrival, she told them all to sit on the ground, tapped on the doorway, and entered.

"Sorry to bother you so early, Garnet. I was out walking and came upon a melee. Jori seemed quite angry with the others."

"The girls were fighting? What happened?" Garnet looked up from the hide she was staining in her lap, her fingers covered with the black walnut juice she used.

"I am not sure. When I came upon them, they were all shouting and rolling around in the grass. I think it had something to do with hunting."

"Jori and Ara planned to stalk rabbits near the garden this morning," Garnet said, wondering if the other girls had done something to disrupt them. She would definitely have to do something about it.

"That is where they were, and I did see two bows," Daña affirmed. "I brought them here for your wise counsel."

"I agree. Let us make their first experience with mediation a memorable one." She looked at her blackened fingers and held one up, smiling mischievously at her friend. "Perhaps the Crone should handle this. I think a little healthy fear is in order. Can you keep them occupied while I prepare?"

"Yes! I will keep them off balance," Daña composed her face and took a deep breath. She took one step out the door and looked at the girls, arms crossed, scowling.

"We were just . . ." Jori started.

"Do not say anything," Daña interrupted the child coldly. "It is not my job to settle disputes."

"But this is not really a dispute," Kelan squeaked.

"No? How did you get that bruise on your chin?"

Kelan touched her face gingerly.

Jori stared intently at her lap.

Daña suppressed a smile.

"Just sit here quietly and wait for the Crone."

"What will she do to us?" Ara, the youngest, showed the greatest fear.

"I do not know. The penalties for attacking a Tribeswoman can be severe," Daña said darkly. "It has not happened in several generations, but I have heard stories about one woman who was left alone in a cave for a whole moon cycle because she fought with others."

Garnet's door opened slowly as if on cue. The girls stared, eyes wide. Daña could not look at Garnet without laughing, so she walked around and stood behind the girls.

Garnet was draped in a dark robe, her face smudged with black, and she held a long walking stick in one hand. The children gasped; even Jori barely recognized her mother. She was bigger somehow and looked so severe.

"Who calls the Crone?" she croaked in a raspy voice.

"These children have a dispute, Mother," Daña announced solemnly. "I found them fighting at the garden."

"FIGHTING?" Garnet's voice boomed, startling the girls.

"Yes," Daña said, masterfully suppressing her laugh.

Garnet looked at Ara, the first child in line. "What have you to say?"

"Um . . . Jori and I were hunting rabbits, and Riala yelled at us and scared them away," Ara said in a rush.

"Riala? Did you spoil the hunt?" the raspy voice of the Crone asked.

"But I did not know they were hunting! They were just lying there looking ridiculous!" Riala whined plaintively.

"Why else would we be lying in the grass at dawn with our hunting tools?" Jori challenged her.

"SILENCE!" Garnet's voice commanded. She pointed at Jori. "I asked you nothing."

The blackened face turned to Kelan. "And why did you hit your Tribe sisters?"

"Jori attacked me, and I defended myself!" Kelan said haughtily.

Garnet's gaze rested silently on the girl. At first Kelan glared back, but as the silence lengthened, she began to fidget. Garnet held her gaze a long moment and then abruptly looked away.

"What was your role in this, Jena?" Garnet demanded.

"I was just out for an early walk with Kelan," her voice quavered, then died as the Crone interrupted.

"Do you know the penalty for saying things that are not true?" Garnet's voice was icy enough to scare even Daña.

"I . . . um . . ." The girl looked very afraid. "We hid and

waited for Riala to yell at them. We were playing a trick on them," she admitted.

"Riala, you planned this?" Garnet asked accusingly.

"They deserved it! They teased me when we fished and made me fall in the water!" She cried plaintively, "We thought it would be funny! We did not know Jori would start a fight!"

With this admission, all the girls began crying or talking.

"ENOUGH!" Garnet silenced them.

"All of you were wrong," she paused, letting the tension build as the silence stretched out. "YOU," she pointed to Kelan, "should know better than to interfere with another woman's activity, whether you approve of it or not. You should have stopped your friends. A leader does not go along with plans she knows are wrong."

Kelan bowed her head.

"And you two," she looked at Riala and Jena, "are just as much at fault as Jori. She may have started the fight, but you joined in readily enough. Since Jori and Ara were trying to keep rabbits from eating our food, you girls will stand watch over the garden and chase hungry rabbits away every morning for the next moon cycle. Now, each of you, report to your mothers what you have done. I will speak with them all before the sun sets."

Kelan, Riala, and Jena rose and skulked away, heads bowed.

"And you two," Garnet said to Jori and Ara, "know better than to ever attack a Tribe sister. Jori, you must learn to control your temper. The Hechtas will decide your punishment. Ara, you will help the Cooks for part of each day for one moon cycle. Extra chores may keep you out of trouble." Her pronouncement had the desired effect. Both girls studied their feet. "Now, Ara, go tell your mother what has happened." Ara rose and trudged toward home.

"Wait here while I remove this robe," she instructed Jori, "then we will go see Marjika."

Garnet saw approval and amusement in Daña's eyes.

"And," she said to Jori, "apologize to Daña for interrupting her walk."

"I am sorry, Daña," Jori said morosely.

Daña patted the child's shoulder. "I will finish it now," she said, winking at Garnet and striding off to the river.

For the next moon cycle, Jori was not allowed to hunt or scout and had to report to the Temple each morning where she was assigned simple, tedious tasks. One of the Hechtas sat beside her as she worked and spoke with her about her duty to the Tribe and the value of controlling her temper.

At first, Jori was miserable. Even in the afternoons when she was free, she sulked around the village. But as the moon cycle progressed, she found that she enjoyed her time with the Hechtas. They seemed to understand her as no one else ever had, save Devin.

On the last day of her punishment, she sat rubbing animal fat into a long piece of wood and listening to Astaga. When Astaga finished her story, Jori summoned her courage and asked a question that had bothered her for weeks.

"Astaga, why must I be Hearth Queen?" She searched for an answer in the woman's eyes.

"You well know it is tradition for daughters of the Queens to follow their mothers' paths."

"But I do not have the talents of a Hearth Queen," Jori protested. "I am terrible with babies; I have little patience for other people's complaints or disputes; I love to hunt and build, and I love to scout and travel," Jori said in a rush. "I am better suited to be Hunt Queen."

"Jori, have faith. I know you have a picture in your head of your future, but perhaps the lesson here is to trust The Mother. She will see that everything turns out as it should," Astaga reassured the girl. "As of today, your punishment for the fight is complete. What have you learned?" she asked.

Jori thought for a moment. "I have learned to have more patience with those who possess less wit or skill than myself."

Astaga smiled in spite of herself. "Go on now, you scamp! Tell your mother I have released you."

Devin made plans for the journey to the Gathering. She, Daña, and Tem gathered necessities for the trip — dried fruits and meats to eat along the trail, soft hides to use as bandages in the event of accidents, and special herbs to keep travelers robust.

Tribeswomen gave Devin trade goods for the festival, to be divided and carried on the backs of travelers or pulled on drags. She was pleased they could offer fur blankets, beautiful pottery, three strong bows, jars of salves made by the Healers, and a few jars of precious salt from a large deposit upriver. Because the meat preserver was harder to find in other places, Wren hoped Devin could trade it for highly prized items such as aromatic spices from the dry lands, especially that one she liked so much called cur–rey.

Garnet decided to stay home and tend her garden. Though she always relished the festive Gatherings, her vision of the Tribe's new way of life depended on the crops and in the end she decided she needed to stay and see to their safety.

After much discussion, both Jori and Kelan were allowed to join the traveling party but none of their friends were going. All of their friends' mothers had elected to stay home themselves and thought their girls too young for such a long trip without them.

Daña, as she had stated at Council, was staying home, as was Lia. Astaga and Nita were going, but the other Hechtas were staying home as well. Wren was going, leaving her apprentice to organize the other Cooks who stayed behind. All told, about half of the Tribeswomen were traveling to the Gathering and half were staying home.

The night before departure, the Cooks prepared a wonderful meal of fish and vegetables, and the Hechtas brought out a keg of wine to celebrate the journey. Barde sang of past journeys to past Gatherings and the many women from other tribes they had met along the way. Petrov and other drummers did not beat out dance rhythms all night as they often did at feasts because the travelers needed to rest. Marjika even gave cups of watered wine to Jori and Kelan to calm their excitement and help them sleep.

Late that night Garnet laid awake, watching her lover breathe deeply in sleep and imagining how she would miss Devin's warmth next to her over the coming weeks. She marveled at hands that were so strong and still so gentle, skilled hands that regularly pulled a bowstring or built a house or peeled the bark off a tree and yet could excite her to frenzy or comfort her like a child.

A tear slid down her cheek when she imagined the lonely nights ahead. Devin usually traveled only a few days, on a hunt or an exploration, and this was the first time since they began lying together that they would be separated for so long.

As Hearth Queen, she believed they had made the right decisions about the Gathering, but as a woman in love, she was bereft at the thought of her partner's absence. She understood now why the she–wolf howled. Garnet always heard the great emptiness in that sound, but never before tonight had she felt it.

She showed no such sadness the next morning as the merry band prepared to leave. She joked with Tem and reassured the children that all would be well until their return. The others who stayed behind took their cue from her, cheering and waving as the travelers began their march downriver.

Several days later under the hot afternoon sun on the trail, no one cheered. Kelan was miserable, and her constant complaining made the rest of the group miserable as well. She was hot and tired; her skin was wet and sticky.

Why did she have to come along anyway? She told Mama she wanted to stay home, but Devin spoke up for the value of the girl's presence and said that a future Hunt Queen would benefit from learning how to manage such a journey and meeting women from other Tribes.

Kelan had no desire whatsoever to meet strangers or learn how much food each woman needed on a long journey. Nonetheless, Devin explained patiently how she calculated the quantity of supplies needed, considering how much fishing or hunting they might do on the way.

To add insult to injury, when they stopped to make camp yesterday Devin told Kelan to help Jori catch fish for dinner! Kelan was embarrassed by her poor fishing skills and repulsed by the slimy scales of the creatures pulled so abruptly from their wet home. Jori tossed many fish onto the bank while Kelan managed only a few and despaired that she might never feel equal to her sister. She trudged along sullenly, so wrapped in her own complaints that she did not hear the voice speaking to her.

"Kelan? Are you awake?" Wren asked loudly.

"Huh? Oh, I am sorry, Wren. What did you ask?"

"Are you all right, dear?" Wren asked, concerned.

"I am tired of walking is all," Kelan said dejectedly, "and my feet ache."

"Well, save your energy, my girl," Wren said merrily, taking the young one's burden from her, "because when we stop for the night, I will show you how to make a travel hearth and prepare dinner on the trail. You will need your strength to gather wood and learn these skills."

As Wren walked off, Kelan sighed her displeasure at the idea of learning to cook. She looked for her mother and found her at the front of the procession.

"Mama, why do I have to learn to cook?" she demanded. "I have never seen you do so."

"Then you have not watched. I take my turn at all tasks when we go out on a hunt or scouting party, and so will you, Kelan. The Hunt Queen must be able to perform any job in the Tribe, including cooking." The girl huffed off.

Devin wondered what she might try next to change her daughter's outlook. She squinted into the distance, away from the river, and saw a Scout running toward them. Devin held her arm up to stop the group, and all took the occasion to sit and rest.

"Devin, I saw a small herd of sheep in some trees not far away," the Scout reported, catching her breath.

Lamb! Devin smiled widely. An excellent meal for the hungry travelers.

"Someone please go find Tem and Jori," she requested and a Hunter responded.

Clasping the Scout's shoulder, she said, "Good job, Swain. We eat well tonight!"

"I will keep an eye on them," the Scout offered, sprinting off, "and leave signs for you to follow."

"Have we found meat?" Tem arrived with a belligerent Kelan in tow and Jori only a step behind.

"Yes! Swain found sheep," Devin's eyes shone in anticipation.

"May I go?" Jori asked excitedly.

"Certainly," Devin nodded and looked at her other daughter. "How about you, Kelan?"

"I prefer to stay here, Mother," the child said hopefully.

Devin sighed and looked at Tem, who shrugged her shoulders.

"All right, then. The rest of you, get your weapons."

Jori quickly strung her little bow and slung her quiver over her shoulder to follow the other Hunters after the Scout. After a short run, they slowed when they saw a signal from Swain. Jori saw sheep grazing on a nearby hill and knew that the wind would soon carry their human scent to the animals.

"Jori," Devin crouched, pulling the girl to her, "you and Swain walk right toward the herd, slowly. Leave your bow and arrows here. Make no attempt to hide yourselves. Tem and I will circle them and hide behind the rocks across the glen. When the sheep smell you, they will come toward us, and we will get one."

"How long should we wait?"

Devin thought a moment. "Sing the Animal Song three times silently, then walk slowly."

Devin and Tem set out to circle the herd, walking softly and crouching so they were hidden by the taller grasses. As they made their arc, Jori noticed that they moved in little spurts with the wind and hid themselves by staying behind the tree line, out of the sheep's vision.

Jori smiled at Swain and whispered the words to the Animal Song three times. The pair stood and slowly walked toward the small herd. Tops of grass blades rubbed Jori's arms, tickling her.

One sheep lifted its head and bleated nervously, causing the entire herd to look up. Jori started to take off on a run, but Swain caught her elbow, cautioning her to walk slowly still.

"We want them to move away, not stampede," Swain said softly. "Make no sudden moves."

Jori nodded and resumed a slow pace. As the pair of humans advanced, the herd kept a constant distance from them, seeming watchful but not about to panic. They just walked away from the danger, though they did stop eating and watched Jori and the Scout closely.

A sudden zing pierced the cool air. Jori was so startled she dropped to the ground on her belly. Embarrassed by her own reflexive move, she scrambled back to her feet in time to see a sheep fall from three arrows in its side. The five sheep still standing ran off.

Swain smirked playfully at the girl, "I see you remember the lesson about dropping in the face of danger."

Jori blushed. "I guess I heard it so many times that now it comes naturally."

Children in the Tribe were taught that whenever danger arose during a hunt, they should just fall to the ground. This eliminated them as a target and kept them out of the line of fire if Hunters had to shoot at a charging animal. Once a child learned to use a bow, she was considered a Hunter and the requirement to drop to the ground ended. But today with no bow in her hand, Jori reverted to her earlier training.

In spite of Swain's gentle chiding, an excited Jori grinned at the other Hunters as they emerged from behind rocks. Fresh meat on the trail! They had traveled many days and were tired of the dried meat strips the Tribe ate when they traveled. Now everyone would enjoy some good meals.

Kelan lifted another branch from the pile and stood it alongside others, building an upside–down cone of fuel for the cooking fire. Earlier, Wren sent women out for sticks and grass. She assigned Kelan to stack it properly and left to supervise preparation of the carcass.

Kelan strongly preferred building the fire to Wren's job. She stood back to review her work. The height was right, as was the shape, so she took the final step of stuffing dry grass into the middle of the sticks. The grass caught easily from the sparks made by the flint and gave the fire its start.

"They will return with the meat soon," Astaga's voice came from behind the girl. "I brought the flint. Would you like to try it?"

The girl's eyes lit up at this rare opportunity. "Oh, yes!" she beamed at the Toolmaker.

Astaga crouched next to Kelan and surveyed her work, poking at the dry grass. "It looks ready. You have done well." She pulled a bag from her waistband and handed it to Kelan.

The Toolmaker silently assessed the girl's skill with the flint. She struck one stone against the other just a few times before the sparks caught on the grass and a little flame shot up, licking the smallest branches. Kelan glanced over her shoulder and saw Astaga's approval. She bent low and blew the little flames which made them surge, and she backed away as the flames rose.

Returning the stones to Astaga, Kelan said, "Thank you for letting me start the fire."

"You did well, Kelan," Astaga smiled. "I know this trip is difficult, but you can enjoy it if you try. You will be a good Queen some day."

"But Astaga, I just hate the idea of being Hunt Queen!" Kelan said dejectedly.

Astaga held the girl's chin with two fingers and looked deeply into her eyes. "Did I say Hunt Queen?"

"But . . . my mother . . . Tradition . . ." Kelan mumbled, confused.

"Kelan," the kindly woman said, "I know the traditions as well as anyone, but let me leave you with a question: How many mothers raised you?"

Astaga rose and walked away from the fire as Wren approached. Kelan stared into the flames and without really understanding why, she felt comforted and hopeful.

"A good job, Kelan," Wren praised her. "We will bring the meat. Please go see if the Hunters need anything. They are bathing in the stream."

The next morning the sun was well up before the women began their day's journey. They took a leisurely breakfast, washed in the river, and repacked items on one of the drags to accommodate the new provisions. It looked to be a fine morning, with a mild breeze blowing toward the rising sun. Jori happily shouldered her burden and marched alongside her sister. Even Kelan seemed better, Jori thought, she is not even complaining.

As was her custom, Swain left camp before sunrise to scout the trail ahead. Jori was still sleeping when Swain left, but when she woke she found a small gift from the Scout next to her bedroll: three arrows with feathers in Swain's colors! Jori hugged them to her, grinning, then placed them carefully in her quiver before she slung it over her shoulder.

Devin sensed restored energy among the women and led them a little faster. Knowing that the terrain would let them cover long distances over the next few days, she asked Barde to sing happy or funny songs to keep spirits high. It seemed to work as no one complained at the faster pace, and at evening fires, the travelers told happy tales and seemed content.

The Scout ran in a few days later to report she had seen the top poles of the Gathering's tents, and they were an easy half-day's journey away. The women were cheered, and they decided to make camp there even though the sun was barely past the middle sky. This way they could start early the next morning and arrive at the Gathering grounds still fresh and rested. Devin sent the Scout ahead to announce their arrival and choose a campsite.

Sitting around the fire after devouring the last of the leftover mutton stew, Devin asked about duty assignments. Those who attended the Gathering performed most of the work involved in creating it. Each Tribe contributed one or more volunteers in each area, ensuring that no one group was overly burdened.

"I know you all told me the Gathering work that you will do back at midsummer so that I could let the Consistory know, but let us go over it again to refresh everyone's memory," Devin explained.

"I will tell Leesa that I will sing one evening," Barde offered, "and I will participate in the group singing on the last night. I love learning new songs from other women!"

"May I help with the children, Mother?" Kelan's face radiated hope.

"I am glad you want to contribute, and I will speak to the child–care workers," Devin said, proud of her daughter's talent with the youngest ones.

"I will assist at the fire," Wren offered as no surprise. Helping the other Cooks gave her an opportunity to trade recipes and spices.

"I will let the Healers know that I am available to assist," Anna added.

"Is anyone teaching a skill?"

"I will teach the Great Bear's fishing method if anyone wants to learn," Tem offered.

"May I help?" Jori jumped up, raising her hand in the air and waving it excitedly, always eager to hunt or fish.

"Of course, little one," Tem smiled. "You may show them how you fish like the Bears, and I will tell them that if a child can do it, anyone can learn!"

The group laughed; Jori looked crushed.

"Of course," Tem said in a conspiratorial tone, "they will not know that you are a better fisherwoman than many of our adult Hunters." She winked merrily at Jori, who brightened considerably.

"When we arrive at the Gathering tomorrow, we go first to the campsite Swain has chosen and unpack. Once we are settled and have set up our camp, we can all go and have fun," Devin grinned. "For now, let us rest. We will be busy all day tomorrow and into the night!"

At early dawn, the group set out with good hearts at a fast pace. They heard drumming and women's voices long before they could see the Gathering's grounds. Laughter flowed and ebbed like a tiny brook in the distance. The closer they came, the louder the noise grew until they finally saw the crowd creating the cacophony of shouting and laughter. The drums boomed so deep and true that the very ground moved with the rhythm, and the closer the Tribeswomen came, the wider they grinned.

Swain walked out to meet them, grinning broadly. "I have found a good spot near the singing ground," she said, leading them in.

A few paces before the edge of the encampment, Devin halted, took a deep breath, and looked at the sky. She felt the vibrations of the big drums through the soles of her tired feet; she smelled wood smoke; she heard the laughter of many women. Touching her amulet, she whispered, "Thank you, Mother, for bringing me here again."

"Devin, look!" Jori shouted, pointing. A tall figure approached, her hair gray at the temples and her black eyes twinkling merrily. Jori ran to her. "Norahjen!"

"Hello, little one!" Norahjen scooped the girl in her arms and swung her up in an arc before setting her back on the ground and giving her a warm hug.

Devin threw her arms around the big Scout. "How are you?"

Norahjen leaned to kiss Devin's cheek and welcomed her Tribe sisters who gathered close. "I am very well but in the middle of final preparations! I cannot linger now, but I will join you at the welcome ceremony later," she promised.

"We will see you at dusk, then," Devin grinned.

Jori watched Norahjen stride through the crowd, taller than any other woman around her.

While Jori had been to Gatherings many times, she was always amazed at the different women and children who attended. Women of every description from many far–away places traveled to meet with other women. The brown women from the deserts across the big water, the sturdy women from the mountains, the little dark–haired women from the north woods, and many others all came together to be with their sisters. Jori did not understand the words that women from other places spoke, but everyone she saw was smiling.

Devin's little troop wound its way around and through many campsites, past the large cleared space called the singing ground, to a grassy spot nearby. Old friends who were busy setting up their own camps greeted them with shouts and waves. Even complete strangers smiled at them. The travelers did not stop to chat, knowing they would see everyone at the opening ceremonies later. They found at their campsite, unloaded packs, and rested briefly before setting up their home for the next few days.

When chores were completed, Tribeswomen left to look for friends, seek a trade, or just look.

Barde went to the singing ground to find Leesa, who arranged the nighttime singing schedule. The singing ground was a large flat area where grass and plants had been worn away long ago by many feet dancing to many a tune. A huge fire circle, too large for a tall woman to leap across, was in the middle, surrounded by boulders as big as a grown woman's head.

Over the next few evenings as soon as it was truly dark, a woman would bring a burning stick from the cooking fires to light the great bonfire, then the singing, dancing, and drumming would begin. Tonight an opening ceremony took place first, after which singing, dancing, and celebration would continue until almost sunrise. Barde could hardly wait.

Finding Leesa near the fire circle, they greeted with a warm hug. "Leesa, my friend, it is so good to see you again."

"Ah, Barde! I was hoping you would arrive today. I heard your Tribe is building a village upriver some days from here."

"Yes, you must come and visit us. Devin and others are building a beautiful home for us."

"Garnet and Devin have talked about this since they were youngsters! I am glad the Tribe consented to try it. Many tribes have permanent villages near the sea, you know," Leesa laughed.

"Yes, Devin has visited there and they have given her many ideas for projects that she wants to try," Barde said proudly of the Hunt Queen. "So, will you have me sing tonight?"

"Of course!" Leesa answered quickly, "The opening ceremony will be blessed by your fine voice. Can you return as the sun sets?"

"Certainly," Barde grinned at the prospect.

"Good. All the other singers and musicians will come as well, and we can greet one another and make plans," Leesa explained.

After sunset, Jori and Kelan sat together at the singing ground in front of the adults, as was the custom. Kelan leaned back on her mother's lap and Jori sat in front of Norahjen, who had joined them as promised. In front of the children's circle lay a wide, cleared space for dancers, and beyond the dance space, a tall fire blazed high above their heads.

There was a chill in the breeze, and Jori leaned against Norahjen to absorb the big woman's warmth. The Scout absentmindedly petted Jori's hair. Women chatted quietly with others around them, occasionally waving to old friends.

Overlooking the scene, the Great Mother tree glistened with newly rubbed oils. She was a huge, forked tree trunk with two legs planted deeply in the earth. Devin told the girls that no one alive, not even Herta, knew how old the Great Mother tree was. She was first placed on the Gathering land generations before. Each year a Rememberer from one Tribe carved a symbol into Her to represent that year's Gathering, and now She was near covered with carvings.

Jori squeezed her eyes closed and tried to imagine how many different tribes had come here over how many seasons. Many symbols on the Great Mother tree were so worn that just a shadow of them remained. Each year, Toolmakers from various tribes oiled, cleaned, and cared for the sculpture.

Breasts, large and small, adorned the entire figure, and Her head had no eyes, nose, or mouth. Norahjen explained that traditionally, representations of The Mother have no face so that every woman can see her own face in The Mother and therefore be reminded that she is the Goddess incarnate. At the figure's feet, the ground was crowded with little carvings, special rocks, and other gifts brought by women to this Gathering.

Jori started to ask another question but was silenced by the sudden sound of loud drums, whistles, and bells. Holding her hands to shield her ears them from the din, she looked around the big circle and saw delight on the faces of every adult and child. Some covered their ears, as Jori did, while others held their hands high in appreciation. Some clapped and whooped. Then just as suddenly as it began, the noise stopped completely. No one moved.

A flash of light and a plume of smoke startled the Gatherers as a figure wearing a dark robe and hood stepped from the smokescreen. She walked slowly and majestically around the fire, her hands raised, palms out, in the ancient sign of greeting for allies. She circled three times, stopping almost directly in front of Jori and Kelan.

Jori looked at her sister and thought she had never before been so beautiful. They had attended the Gathering many times, but never before had Kelan seemed so drawn in to the ritual.

Jori's attention was drawn back to the circle as the tall woman dropped her robe, revealing her naked body covered with many painted symbols. Jori saw that her thin body was strong and beautiful, and she had just one breast. She walked around the fire until she faced the direction of the sunrise. When she spoke, her melodious voice soothed Jori's ears. It was gentle and seemed quiet, but could be heard by all in the circle.

"Hail to thee, sisters from the lands of the rising sun! Welcome to the circle of The Mother. Welcome home."

She moved partway around the fire and continued, "Hail to thee, sisters from the hot sands! Welcome to the circle of The Mother! Welcome home."

Again she moved and spoke, "Hail to thee, sisters from the lands of the setting sun. Welcome to the circle of The Mother. Welcome home."

And finally, "Hail to thee, sisters from the lands of cold winds. Welcome to the circle of The Mother. Welcome home."

Walking around the circle slowly, looking at each woman and child, she continued, "Each summer, we gather to honor our Mother and to celebrate and learn from one another. We share work, laughter, and our skills and beliefs. We share food, music, and the love in our hearts. We do this to affirm that which our ancestors have always known: No matter where we come from or what our customs, we are all daughters of The Mother, and so we are all sisters. Take now your sister's hand and join the circle." She paused as women and girls around the circle took each others' hands. "Feel yourself connected with all women, with all life. Feel yourself as one with all that is."

They sat in silence, the crackling fire the only sound. The ritual leader continued slowly around the circle, looking again at each woman and child. When her gaze fell on Kelan, she stopped a moment. Kelan looked into the woman's warm, brown eyes and felt an instant kinship. The woman smiled deeply at Kelan before she moved on.

"Let us sing the Ancestors' Chant."

Everyone joined in, softly at first, gaining volume and speed with repetition, "We are you, you are we; all is one, within me." Drummers beat a cadence and the women matched it, their chant growing louder and their voices more joyful.

Jori saw Kelan's eyes closed in concentration as she spoke ancient words of connection, and she felt a warm tingling in her palm where they held hands. Kelan's face seemed to blur and change. First, she resembled the woman in the circle, then Jori's mother, then a woman Jori had never seen before. Jori blinked her eyes and looked at Kelan again to see only Kelan.

As its volume increased, the chant gained power. The leader's voice could still be heard over the chants and drums, even though she spoke in a gentle way.

"My sisters, as we raise the spirits of our mothers, as we connect with our sisters, may we be blessed and loving. May our days be long and our children happy," she said. "Blessed be!"

"Blessed be!" answered the women, ending the chant. They unclasped hands and reached to the sky, smiling.

Entertainment followed the welcome ritual: singers, harpers, dancers, drummers, and storytellers, even a pair of women with big carved masks who stood as tall as the trees. Devin called them "stilt walkers," and Jori wondered how they kept their balance on those big sticks. She wanted to find them the next day and see if they might teach her.

Over the next four days, Jori learned interesting new ideas and skills, attending at least one lesson each afternoon with Devin and Kelan. One Tribe taught how they made traps for small animals and another shared their unique system of decision–making.

They walked through the market place each day, seeing useful tools and beautiful creations from many places, and they made mental notes of items to trade for later.

The many women and girls of all colors, ages, shapes, and sizes excited them most. Jori was especially curious about others' customs and looked forward to sharing with her mother the new ideas she learned. She missed Garnet's gentle presence and her beautiful smile.

Garnet thought of her traveling family, too. She felt lonely for her girls and Devin, but she was in the midst of an even deeper loss. She sat on a stump, a warm blanket wrapped around her, the fire blazing hotly between her and the Temple. Closest to the fire, her feet were warm, but she felt the contrast of a cool breeze on her face.

Marjika and Herta sat nearby, both Hechtas focused on the tasks before them and respecting Garnet's need for silence. They gave her restorative tea and a blanket, but that was all she took from them.

The Hechtas knew how deeply Garnet experienced the loss of any Tribe member, especially a child. On occasions in the past when a baby had not survived, she usually took long walks in the woods with Devin to grieve, but in Devin's absence, the Hechtas did what they could to comfort her.

Garnet reviewed all that had happened since this ordeal began. Just after sunset the night before, Adriana began to have pains. Knowing it was moons too soon, Garnet helped the young woman into bed and sent for Lia.

The two stayed with Adriana all night and into the morning, offering restoratives, herbs, and other techniques to ease her pain and help the baby. Despite all their efforts, Adriana's body finally shuddered and convulsed in labor, and she delivered the child stillborn.

Lia and Garnet stayed with Adriana until she slept deeply from a tea that Lia gave her. As they left, Lia guided Garnet into her own house and made tea for her, then sat with Garnet and cradled her as she wept.

"There, there my love," Lia crooned softly, gently stroking her hair. "The Mother knows best in these matters."

"Oh, Lia!" Garnet sobbed, "It is so sad! Poor Adriana."

"She is young and will bear more children. I looked at this one before we buried it, and his death was a blessing," Lia's tone was solemn.

Exhausted, Garnet rested her head on Lia's shoulder. "Why?"

"He was not whole," Lia said, refusing to explain any more.

"And what of Adriana?"

"After the grief from her loss passes, she will be fine. I saw no damage to her birthing parts. She will stay in the Temple through her time of darkness, and the Hechtas will help her grieve and heal."

Drying her eyes, Garnet said, "Thank you for listening. I needed a friend right now."

"I am always here for you." Lia said, leaning over and kissing Garnet on the mouth.

Garnet jerked back, stunned. "No, I . . ." she sputtered.

"It is all right, my love. It often takes a crisis to show us what we truly feel," Lia smiled at her warmly, leaning toward her again.

"What?" Now Garnet was truly angry. "What do you think I feel?"

"Why, our connection. Do not tell me you do not feel it!" Lia exclaimed, truly perplexed by Garnet's sudden anger.

"All I feel is despondence over our loss of a child, and I sought comfort from a friend!" Garnet now saw nothing beyond her own rage. "Anything else is only in your imagination, Lia. I have no interest in more!"

"But Garnet, I . . ." Lia sobbed, reaching toward the woman.

"I am leaving. Do not speak of this again, Lia. It is not healthy for you to carry on about an attraction when the feelings are not returned. You must stop!" Garnet stormed out.

Herta looked up from the hide she was curing to see Garnet angrily sling the remnants of her tea into the fire. Even now, after a quick walk and sitting safely here with the Hechtas, she still felt shock and wondered if she should tell the wise women the entire story. Lia did seem obsessed with her, but she thought perhaps she should keep this private matter to herself for the good of all. Gossip never helped. Still, the Hechtas were her spiritual partners, integral to helping her look after the Tribe's health. Finally resolved, she told them about the unpleasant encounter.

"Yes, I thought she looked at you like a lovesick child," Herta offered.

"This cannot affect the Tribe. Lia is a good Healer, and women must believe in her if she is to do her work."

"Yes," Marjika spoke softly to the Queen, "I agree. We must not cause doubt. Do you think we should invite Lia to the Temple for counseling?"

"No," Garnet sighed heavily and shook her head, "let us just wait and see. Maybe the emotion of the moment confused her. She has never behaved like this before."

"As you wish," Nita's tone betrayed her reluctance, "but we will watch more closely now that we know."

On the Gathering's third day, Devin encountered her dear friend, Ubakala. Devin told her enthusiastically of their new village and invited Ubakala to visit so she could see for herself.

Ubakala laughed and said she had already traveled an entire moon from her homelands to the Gathering. If she traveled farther toward the cold mountains, she would never get home before winter began! Ubakala's dark skin was accustomed to dry sand and hot sun, and she felt like winter began when the first leaves fell.

Jori stared at the long and sinewy woman whose muscles stood out even when she relaxed. Her skin was brown as a summer berry. She is so beautiful, Jori thought.

Ubakala's family joined them for that evening's meal, and Jori saw that they did not eat meat. Ubakala explained that, while her people understood that sometimes an animal's life had to be taken in order to survive, they preferred not to kill animals if they could avoid it. Because the Gathering offered women plenty of grains, fruits, and vegetables, Ubakala's Tribeswomen did not have to eat animals there.

After dinner, Kelan sat with two children who showed her how to play a game with a little hoop and several polished stones. Devin was happy to see Kelan enjoying herself so.

"Your daughter is so good with children!" Ubakala commented.

"Yes, I saw her minding a whole herd of them yesterday. They all ran and played, but when she spoke, they all listened. I would have been overwhelmed by so much ruckus, but she seemed to enjoy it," Devin replied.

"Jori is a strong one, too. I saw her making spears yesterday. She will make a fine Hunt Queen," Ubakala told her friend.

"Yes, she would," Devin's head dropped dejectedly, "but Jori is Garnet's daughter and so is expected to become Hearth Queen. I am afraid both girls will be unhappy when time comes for them to take their traditional places."

"Ahhh, my friend, your Tribe highly respects a woman's talents and individual choices. I think it will be all right," Ubakala's brown eyes comforted her friend. "They will be fine."

"How do you know?" Devin looked up hopefully. "It is custom and the Tribe expects it."

"Trust the wisdom of the Tribe and the love of The Mother. All will be well. I know inside."

"I have always trusted your intuition, my friend." Relief washed over Devin.

On the Gathering's last day, Tem taught a curious group the Bear Mother's fishing method, beginning with the tale of how She gave the Tribe this important gift. The Hunters sat in a circle, legs crossed, and listened to Tem.

"Garnet and Devin walked along the river, following Devin's mother and the Scouts, looking for roots we use for healing. As they came around a bend in the river, there, in the water, stood a Mother Bear with two cubs."

Tem knew this was not exactly how young Garnet and Devin had encountered the Bear, but she dramatized a little for the sake of a good story. "The Queen signaled to stop and be quiet, and all crouched in the grass to watch. The Mother Bear stood and looked at them, her head swaying back and forth. They expected Her to charge them, but after studying them a bit, She went back to Her fishing."

With the Hunters' rapt attention, Tem continued, "Mother Bear stood very still, Her great paws dangling in the water. A fish swam between Her paws, and quick as lightning She scooped it up and threw it onto the bank. The cubs ate the fish almost as quickly! It was fascinating. After eating a few fish, the larger cub waded into the water and tried to catch some on its own. At first, it just splashed around clumsily, but soon enough, the cub got one."

The crowd murmured appreciatively at the story.

"The small party went home and told the Hunters all about

the lesson that the Bear Mother had given them. The next day, we all went to the river to try it out. Even though I was just a child, I remember as if it were yesterday. That first time, we managed to get only a few fish. Devin's mother insisted we offer our first catch to the Mother Bear and Her cubs, to thank Her for the lesson. We walked downriver to the Bears' place, and there they were again.

"Devin asked if she could take the offering to the Bear and, though her mother was concerned at the danger, the child was not to be denied. Small as she was, Devin showed no fear at all! She walked to the edge of the river and set down the fish. We all backed away. The Bear Mother walked over cautiously and picked up the offering. She looked right into Devin's eyes and growled loudly! I think She said, "Thank you." I will never forget seeing Devin stand before Her, looking so bravely into those warm, black eyes. The Mother Bear seemed very kind," she paused and smiled.

"Ever since that day," she went on, "many of our Tribe have used the Bear Mother's method to catch fish. Each spring we take our first catch and offer it to the Bears with our thanks."

"Now," she said, rising to her feet, "let us try it. Jori is skilled at the Bear's fishing ways. She will demonstrate."

The Hunters were excited to try this kind of fishing as they hiked the short distance to the river. Once in the water, they watched Jori catch a few fish and then tried it themselves. Right away, Jori noticed that the smaller women had quicker hands and caught more fish. All the Hunters were amazed at her ability, though she thought it quite natural.

As Hunters practiced, Jori and Tem walked along the bank offering advice and encouragement. Many Hunters could catch a fish or two after a few attempts, but none caught as many as Jori, not even Tem.

Students and teachers alike enjoyed the outing, and soon their laughter and playful splashing scared away any fish within miles. But by that time, they had caught more than sufficient for the afternoon Gathering meal so that travelers could also take succulent leftovers on their journeys home. But first, the Hunters took some of their catch downriver for The Mother, asking the smallest woman in the class to place the fish there.

Music and merriment always filled the Gathering's final night. Each Tribe offered a song for all to sing, and each also expressed gratitude for a happy Gathering and their wishes for the coming seasons.

Near the end of the evening's celebrations, a woman stood and held up her hands for silence. Jori recognized the same woman from the opening ritual.

"Thank you, my sisters, for coming here once again and sharing yourselves with one another," she said. "We wish to honor one among you who has proven herself a skilled Hunter and a patient teacher." When the woman walked to Jori and motioned for her to rise, Jori's heart leapt. Could it be true? The Gathering was honoring her?

"Today this girl helped teach a new skill to many Hunters. At her young age when few children give a thought to important skills, she has so mastered the skills involved in this new way of catching fish that today she helped a Hunter teach others. Her Tribe learned this method from the Bear Mother, who they revere. The most respected Hunters told me that she caught more fish today than any other. She offered her catch to feed us all, except for a portion that was taken downstream to offer the Bear Mother.

"Later this afternoon, women from several Tribes made this amulet for her to show our esteem for her skills and courage. May all who see it remember that abundance and prosperity come from giving to and sharing with your sisters." She took the amulet from around her own neck and slipped it over Jori's head. It was a small stone carving of a Mother Bear!

The crowd exploded with cheers and whoops! Jori blushed and fidgeted, uncomfortable at the attention, and Norahjen placed a reassuring hand on the girl's shoulder.

"Will you lead us in the closing song, child?" The ritual leader looked kindly at Jori and smiled. Jori looked to Devin, who nodded.

Jori sang the ancient Song of Parting which she had learned at past Gatherings. All joined hands and sang:

> May the circle be opened, but unbroken,
> May the love of The Mother be ever in our hearts!
> Merry meet, and merry part, and merry meet again.

After they sang this chorus three times, all hands went into the air as everyone shouted, "MERRY MEET AND MERRY PART AND MERRY MEET AGAIN! HEY!"

Days later, Garnet sat working at the garden, still sad at Adrianna's and the Tribe's recent loss. Her thoughts were interrupted by a familiar voice.

"Mother! Mother!" Jori's voice rang out as she ran toward home. Garnet saw the child. Why was she alone? And so alarmed? She dropped her digging tool and sprinted to her daughter.

"What is it, child? Where is the rest of the party?" The girl fell breathlessly into her mother's arms. Daña walked up, having heard the commotion.

"What has happened?"

"It is Devin," Jori gasped between breaths, "and Anna! They are hurt. We need Lia and Mother!"

"Jori, what happened? How are they hurt?" Garnet ex–claimed.

"Anna fell into the water as she crossed the river, and the current carried her downstream. Devin ran down the bank, jumped in, and saved her, but Devin hurt her leg. Anna does not wake up, though she still breathes. Tem said Anna must have hit her head on a rock, and she asks you to come quickly." The story tumbled out in a rush now that Jori had regained her breath.

"How far downriver?" Daña asked, calm as ever though worry showed clearly in her face.

"I was early morning when I left. The sun was not over the mountains yet."

"Good. We should be able to reach them before sunset," Daña said.

"You have done well, my daughter. Go tell the Hechtas so they may care for you until we return." Garnet hugged her daughter close.

Daña went in search of Lia and her herbs; Garnet desperately held on to her composure. She went to a storage house and got two drags that leaned against a wall. She returned to the village center just as Daña arrived with Lia, and the three women ran downstream.

Garnet's mind raced with worry. She pictured Devin jumping into the rapids, her only thought to save Anna. Garnet willed herself to calm, chanting over and over in her head, "They are all right. They are all right."

Her legs and feet ached from relentless pounding across the ground, and the hot sun beat mercilessly on them, forcing them to stop at times to rest and drink water. At these stops, Lia made Garnet rest until she regained her breath, telling the leader that she would be no good to anyone if she did not care for herself.

They finally spotted the Gathering party just as the sun began to set. A fire had been lit and two figures lay nearby, one propped up to a sitting position.

Garnet rushed to Devin's side and touched her face tenderly and tearfully. Lia went immediately to Anna and examined her. Daña sought Tem to ask how she could help.

"What happened? How badly hurt are you?"

"I am sorry to frighten you, darling. It is my leg. Tem thinks I have a broken bone. Kelan cleaned the dirt out of my cuts. She has stayed at Anna's side and kept her warm." Tight lines around Devin's mouth told Garnet she was in great pain in spite her brave front. Garnet felt reassured that Devin was alert enough to worry about the group's morale.

Feeling along Devin's leg for the position of the bone, she confirmed that it was broken, but fortunately, the bone had stayed inside the skin. Garnet had seen a broken bone once that tore through skin, and the break never healed well. This one would; Garnet willed it so.

"I will give you something to ease the pain," Garnet kissed her gently.

"See to the camp first, love. I am all right," Devin whispered, "but they need you to take charge."

Garnet rested her forehead on Devin's chest. "I know," Devin said quietly. "Now, go."

Garnet stood and looked where Anna lay. Kelan and Lia sat next to her, talking. Lia moved to the cooking fire.

Daña appeared at Garnet's side with two straight branches and strips of hide. "I will strip the bark off these branches so they will be more comfortable against Devin's leg," she said.

Reassured that Devin was being cared for, Garnet went to Anna's side and asked Kelan, "How is she?"

"Still not awake. Lia brews something that smells awful. She said the odor alone should startle Anna awake." Kelan glanced at her mother and smiled. "It will take a while for the water to boil. I will stay with Anna if you want to go to Devin and care for her leg." Garnet was impressed by the girl's competent and calm manner. Kelan had matters well in hand. She accepted Kelan's suggestion with a nod and returned to Devin.

"Kelan and Lia are caring for Anna," she reassured Daña. "Let us bind this leg and then I will see to travel preparations."

Positioning themselves carefully and holding Devin's leg

gently, they pulled the limb until Garnet's sensitive hands could feel the bones straighten. While Tem continued to pull the leg gently to keep the broken bone in place, Garnet held the two branches on either side of the injured leg, and Daña wrapped hide strips firmly but not too tightly around it. Devin squeezed Garnet's hand when Daña tightened the strips. Their eyes met, and Garnet expressed all of her love and concern in silence. Devin felt better and smiled.

Garnet turned to Lia and asked, "What can we do for Anna?"

"I have brewed something to jar her awake. Come cradle her head while I hold this under her nose, but take care not to inhale the fumes yourself. They are quite harsh." Lia held the gourd as far away as she could from her own nose and walked carefully.

Garnet followed the Healer to Anna's side where she knelt and lifted Anna to a position where she half sat, half laid on Garnet's lap. Garnet smiled at Kelan, who looked tired and concerned.

"Good," Lia instructed, "now turn your head away." Garnet did as told, but still the sharp, angry smell entered her nostrils when Lia held the bowl right under poor Anna's nose.

Almost immediately, Anna began to sputter. "Come on," Lia encouraged, "open your eyes." Anna coughed and her eyes opened, still unfocused. Lia moved the bowl away.

"Wha . . .? Where . . .?" Anna mumbled, looking around. "Garnet? Lia?"

"We are here, dear one." Garnet gently lay her down onto a grass– stuffed pillow.

Lia felt the woman's forehead. "Do you know what happened?"

The woman squinted in concentration. "I . . . fell in the water . . .?" she said uncertainly.

"Yes, you did, and Devin pulled you out," Garnet said softly. "Are you dizzy?"

"No, just foggy and sore."

"Do you hurt anywhere besides your head?"

"My elbow," Anna said, trying to hold up her arm.

Lia inspected carefully. "There is no break, but a lot of skin is scraped off. We will put on some salve and a covering. Keep her talking, Garnet. I will be right back."

Lia walked a little ways away from the camp to dump the bitter brew, then went to the fire to brew a restorative for Anna. She asked Kelan to get salve from her pack and take it to Garnet. Kelan did as asked and returned to Garnet and Anna.

"I can apply the salve, Mother, and the bandage," Kelan offered.

Garnet nodded for the girl to proceed. She spoke quietly to Anna as Kelan cleaned the wound, applied the salve gently, and wrapped the wound in strips of clean hide.

"Well done, daughter," Garnet smiled encouragingly at the girl. "Please ask Lia for some of that tea she is brewing."

"Yes, Mama," the girl smiled shyly and went to find Lia.

Others from the village arrived to help carry the injured women home, and Garnet called all the women to the fire.

"Thank you all for your concern and help," she said warmly. "Lia tells me it is safe to spend the night here before we take Devin and Anna home, and after the day we have all had, I must agree we need to rest. In the morning, we will put both injured women onto drags. We must not jostle them more than necessary, so we have to carry the drags. Four women are needed for each drag, to take turns in pairs. Daña will organize you. The rest of you, please pack up everything and be ready to return home at first light. Do not wait for us." She looked around for Kelan, finding her still sitting with Anna.

"Kelan, can you find the village from here?" she asked the child gently.

"Of course," Kelan replied, tossing her hair and rolling her eyes at the unnecessary question. Garnet smiled at Kelan's return to acting more like her young self.

"You have done very well, my daughter." The assembled women murmured agreement and praise for the girl. Good, Garnet thought. The Tribeswomen needed to trust her. "Please lead the party home tomorrow morning. I will return with Devin and Anna."

Garnet awoke at first light, smiling. She had rolled over in the night and slept with her head on Devin's chest, just as she did at home.

"Good morning, beautiful one." The customary greeting made Garnet's heart soar.

She kissed Devin, "Good morning, yourself."

"Everyone else is up already. What is the plan?"

"Kelan will lead the party home ahead of us, and some of us will take turns carrying you and Anna on drags. We have to go slowly. Neither one of you should be banged about."

"Kelan has done very well," Devin looked at her lover hope–fully, "has she not?"

"She has," Garnet assured her. "I know you have been concerned about her. Sometimes it takes an emergency to show what a person can do, and believe me, she handled this crisis as well as you would have."

"I need a word with Tem," Devin said.

Garnet sat up and looked around. Women bustled about, packing gear and preparing for the final leg of their journey home. Garnet spotted Tem and waved her over.

"Let Kelan lead the party, Tem," Devin said quietly, "but

please also watch discreetly that she leads in the right direction."

"Just as I have always done for you since we were children," Tem grinned broadly. Devin laughed; Garnet scowled.

Patting Garnet's hand, Tem assured, "Do not worry, Garnet. I am teasing. Kelan will do just fine."

Garnet smiled meekly. "I know, Tem. I am just preoccupied with worry. I appreciate your support."

The women in the first party soon began their trek upriver with Kelan in the lead. They carried everything that had to be taken home, save the two drags for the injured women and a small amount of food and utensils.

The remaining women picked up the drags and began their careful trek home. Garnet was grateful for the mild weather and the cool breeze.

During the slow walk to the village, Garnet learned that Kelan had played a key role early in the crisis.

Herta and other women told the story of how Kelan took charge after everyone was out of the water. She told them all to take off their wet clothes and asked one of the hunters to start a big fire. She told those who were not injured to wrap themselves in sleeping furs while their clothes dried, and she asked for hot tea to be brewed. Kelan carefully stripped off Anna's clothes, wrapped her in sleeping furs, and made a pillow for her head.

She asked several women to carry Devin to the fire. When they laid Devin down, she stripped her clothes, too. She sent for Anna's medicine sack and retrieved a salve, then she washed and bandaged the scrapes and cuts on Devin's body and applied the salve gently. Once that was done, she checked everyone else for minor cuts and scrapes.

Garnet was proud of both her daughters' intelligent and mature responses to the crisis. Neither panicked nor fell apart under the pressure.

Garnet saw Jori leading women from the village out to meet

them. Many hands took over carrying the drags, and some women brought food and water for those who had already carried their precious cargo a long distance.

Jori went straight to Devin, her face lined with worry. She held Devin's hand a moment and breathed in relief when she saw Devin smile. She laid her forehead on Devin's arm, then turned to Garnet.

"Do not be afraid, Mama. The Hechtas have done protective 'majik', and besides, Devin is strong and will heal. Kelan and I will help with her duties until she can walk again."

Garnet smiled at the child. She sounded so protective and grown up! "I never have to fear for anything so long as you are here, my love," she said, squeezing the girl's hand. Jori's shoulders straightened and she stood a little taller.

"The Hechtas have prepared a place for Anna and Devin in the Tribe house, Mother, and Diana built a fire in the hearth to keep them warm," Jori said. Diana was Wren's apprentice.

"That was smart of the Hechtas," her mother said. "With Anna and Devin together, one woman can tend them both. And it was kind of Diana to start a fire."

"Everyone wanted to help in some way," Jori's matter–of–fact tone made Garnet smile.

"Of course. It is natural to want to help when someone has been hurt."

The party took the two injured women directly to the Tribe house, where they found Diana tending the fire and boiling water for tea. The women laid Devin and Anna on beds of dried grass, and Devin sat up with the help of a backrest.

Every woman and child in the Tribe was in and around the house, all greeting their arriving Tribemates and talking loudly.

"Please!" Lia shouted above the din. "Please, everyone, quiet down! Even though Anna is awake now, she needs quiet and rest."

"Lia is right," Garnet agreed. "I know everyone wants to hear stories of the accident and the Gathering. Let us all sit down and ask the travelers to tell us together what happened."

"Come," Wren started toward the door, pulling Diana, "let us make tea for everyone and bring some snacks as well. I will tell you what happened to Anna and Devin as we work." Wren and a small group left the big house.

"Barde?" Garnet looked for the singer. "Will you begin by telling us how Anna and Devin were injured? We will hear stories from the Gathering later."

. The Singer stood. "We were on our way home, and all were in good spirits. In late morning, Anna said she saw kartof on the other side of the river and wanted to get some for dinner. She found what looked like a good crossing place with stones all the way across shallow water. She stepped from one stone to the other, but one was covered with moss, and she slipped and hit her head. Jori heard her fall and called out to the rest of us because we had not seen."

"The current was strong. Before we could even move, the river had pulled Anna under and carried her downstream," she paused for her listeners to breathe. "I thought she would surely die, but Devin dropped her pack, ran down the riverbank, and jumped in. She pulled Anna's head out of the water and held her up. Anna was bleeding badly. She woke and started to struggle, not understanding that Devin was saving her, and she knocked Devin down."

Women and girls leaned forward. "The water was chest–high and running fast, but Devin struggled to her feet again. By then, Tem and Wren had also jumped in, and they helped pull Anna to the bank. Anna seemed not to know them. Her struggling made them all fall again! Others of us lay on the bank and reached down to pull them all up, one at a time.

"After everyone was out of the water, we all laid there until we got our breath. Anna was not awake, so Kelan quickly rolled her onto her belly and pressed on her back until Anna choked out some water. She coughed, but she still did not wake. Devin told Jori to run to the village for help, then she tried to stand up but fell right down. She almost slipped back into the water, but Tem grabbed her arms and pulled her higher onto the bank. That is when we realized that Devin was injured, too."

Garnet watched Barde talk and admired how her tone of voice and gestures brought the tale alive; the entire Tribe waited on every word.

"Kelan organized us. She asked me to make a fire, and she had us get the clothes off everyone who was wet. She asked others to gather grass and leaves for Anna and Devin to lie on. Everyone helped, but Kelan took charge and seemed to know what to do."

Many eyes looked at Kelan, who smiled shyly and said, "Ummmm, everyone helped."

"Such a modest child!" Barde smiled proudly at her. "By the time Garnet and Lia arrived, Kelan had settled the injured women and tended to Devin's scrapes and cuts. She made sure no one was cold or wet or bleeding. Wren fixed tea and food for us as soon as she dried herself."

"We are proud of you all," Garnet commented. "Our Tribe's strength comes from everyone working together."

"I am thankful," Devin spoke for the first time, slowly but with a strong voice, "for all of you. Without your assistance, I would still be out there trying to walk home, or worse."

"I feel responsible," Anna said softly. "If I had not slipped on that rock, none of this would have happened."

"But you were trying to gather food," Jori said comfortingly. "You were hurt accidentally because you were taking care of us. There is no fault in that."

Sounds of assent moved through the crowd. Jori was right. All were happy that the Healer had survived at all.

Eventually, talk turned from the injuries to the Gathering.

Women and children sat together into the night, hearing stories of all that was seen, heard, and done by the travelers. Barde sang new songs she had learned. As the dark turned into early light, the children and then the women straggled off to their beds, all except Garnet, who smiled the rest of the night away with her head on Devin's shoulder.

Lia found them that way when she entered the Tribe house soon after sunrise. "I need to check the bandages," she explained.

Garnet hovered while the Healer worked, making conversation that she hoped would distract Devin from pain. "Daña says Anna should be on her feet in a few days."

"Yes, I think so, too," Lia agreed without looking up. "She seems to be doing well."

Garnet turned to Anna's reclining form. "How are you feeling, dear?"

"Sore," Anna grimaced as she pushed herself to a sitting position, "but my head is clear. That feels good."

"You, however," Lia said to Devin as she finished her task, "must stay completely off of this leg for a long time."

"I cannot!" Devin worried aloud. "I must take parties out for supplies!"

"The garden grows well, dear," Garnet reassured her. "We are already eating some of its food."

"I promised the Elders that we would have enough in storage to last all winter, and we need enough to trade the men for their work!"

"Why not let Kelan lead parties out?" Anna asked.

"She has certainly proven she is capable," Tem spoke up from the doorway. No one had heard the Hunter enter. "I can watch over her to make sure she is safe."

"Jori can help," Garnet offered.

"Perhaps I can go if . . ." Devin began.

"It will not help the Tribe if you walk on it too soon and never walk right again," Lia scolded.

"You cannot risk your health!" Garnet blurted at the same moment.

Devin grumbled, "I suppose," as Garnet traded a knowing look with Tem and the Healers.

Kelan was no happier with the plan than Devin, but for different reasons.

"Why must I lead parties?" Kelan cried indignantly when she was told.

"For many reasons . . ." Devin tried to stay reasonable with the girl, but her patience wore thin. "You are the next Hunt Queen, the Tribe must learn to trust you, and because I ask it."

Kelan made a rude noise. "I do not WANT to be Hunt Queen! I do not WANT to lead the Hunters!"

"Dear one, I know this seems too big a job for you, but Tem will go on every trip and help."

"Why can Tem not lead the parties? And what about hunting? What if I faint again at the sight of a kill?" Kelan whined.

"Tem can indeed lead the parties, but I am not asking her to. She is not my daughter. You are, and I ask you to do this," Devin's anger showed in her voice. "You sound selfish and childish, Kelan, not like the mature young woman who took charge so well when Anna and I were injured. You must think of the Tribe now, not your own desires."

Kelan began crying and stormed out of the house. Devin called to her but she would not come back. Devin was at her wits' end with the child. How could she ever get the girl to understand the importance of her duties to the Tribe? She called to Garnet, hovering nearby in case she was needed.

"Did you hear all of that? Should we go after her?" Devin asked miserably.

"I do not think so, darling," Garnet said, sitting next to Devin and pulling her lover's weary head to her soft lap. "You must let her express her feelings."

"The trouble is that she is right. Jori is the one to lead the Hunters."

"Kelan is capable as well, dear," Garnet said.

"Yes, and I would not hesitate to let her take your place in the Tribe, but she hates to hunt and gather, and her unhappiness affects everyone else."

"You are right. We must find a way to convince the Tribe that we must all honor the children's sacred choices!" Garnet said passionately. "They deserve to be happy, too. Perhaps if more women see how unhappy Kelan is in the Hunt Queen role . . ."

And so each morning a handful of Hunters pulling empty drags followed Kelan out of the village, and each afternoon they returned, drags full of the plants and other foods gathered that day. Many hands stayed busy in the village drying fruits, herbs, and grinding grain.

Jori was assigned to take a troop of girls to the river to fish and gather roots and plants that grew in the river's shallows, and Daña accompanied them to ensure their safety. Jori sang and whistled as she led her party out at first light each day, in stark contrast to Kelan's sullen manner.

The Hechtas and the Healers made special mixtures with the water plants the girls gathered. Astaga taught Jori that liquid from the roots of one plant could be used to preserve tools made from bone, preventing them from drying out and becoming brittle. To keep the tools strong enough to use, they had to be periodically rubbed with the plant's juices.

Each afternoon, the Cooks smoked the day's catch of fish over the new hearth fire and raved over how well this inside fire worked.

Garnet walked to her garden each day to see the plants' progress. Lettuce and early onions had ripened already and were harvested. Jori and other children carried the garden's bounty to the Cooks each day for preserving or preparation.

As the storage houses filled, Kelan's resentment grew towards the changes she knew were coming. She felt sorry for herself that other children could still play while she had to lead the Hunters. She complained regularly to her mother and Garnet until they tired of her noise and put a stop to it.

Thereafter, she sulked silently, speaking to others only when necessary.

Summer
1984 C.E.

Sweat poured down the sides of my face and burned my eyes. The sun was up and the day was hot. My chore at the moment was to turn a spit with a chicken roasting over the blazing hearth fire.

Aranna came out of the cabin carrying her slicing knife and a bowl of beets and onions. The old rocking chair creaked its objection as she sat down to her work. Watching her instead of my own business, I reached too far into the fire and the flame seared my hand. I jerked back and roared like a grizzly, waving my hand through the air to cool it and cursing loudly.

She called me to her and took my injured paw gently between her own healing hands. Smiling as she inspected the red, angry place on my wrist, she told me to close my eyes. I did and felt the cool air of her breath wafting over the burn. I concentrated on the coolness; the pain receded. She patted my arm and let go. I opened my eyes and looked at my wrist only to see no evidence at all of injury.

She often performed similar little 'majiks'. I wasn't astounded so much by her talents, but rather by the matter–of–fact way she utilized them. She did not show off, she simply did what she knew to do in any given situation.

Another day, I made her weep. It came so suddenly and was so powerful that I felt scared silly. I sat with her, mumbling and fumbling incompetently, trying to give her a handkerchief. She had been telling me about the Summer Gathering of Sisters, which I said brought to mind a modern–day gathering I always attended in the northern woods of the U.S.

"Tell me about your 'Meh–shee–gan,'" she asked leaning forward, eyes sparkling.

Every year, I told her, women from all over the world gather in the woods of northwest Michigan to build a village. I told of amazing music into the night and wonderful workshops all day long where women could learn everything from spiritual lessons to solar power instructions from other women; I raved about the yummy, all–vegetarian meals prepared for thousands; and I complained about the damn cold showers back in the days before the festival installed solar water heaters.

She asked about the drumming, the magic, the tractors, and the women who put all this together. Her joyful tears flowed freely when I told her of a statue of the Goddess that women created over many years with loving carvings and hand–made decorations; how one year She was hit by lightning and only Her head survived. Some women cherished and cared for the Goddess's head, taking Her home, keeping Her safe, oiling Her, and placing Her carefully on the ground in the same sacred circle year after year. Through her tears, Aranna said those women were kin to Astaga, descendants of the original Keepers of the Relics.

I learned that there are many ways we keep the Tribe's traditions alive today. Like Aranna, we all have our own little 'majiks' that we take for granted. We don't consciously understand that we are keeping millennia–old traditions. We simply experience cravings – to light the candles, to light the bonfires, to state the reality we wish to create, to acknowledge the changes of the seasons, and sometimes to gather and do these things together.

In those woods with her, I began to understand that there are women today descended from the Tribe. I believe that we hold a kind of collective memory of who we were and are, and that memory drives us to gatherings and festivals and other women's spaces.

I believe that once we all belonged to something together, and in its absence, we search for ways to belong again. We find our Tribe in Dianic ritual circles and at festivals, women's concerts, even coffee houses. I think we simply miss one another. Over my lifetime I have met women with whom I shared an instant sense of familiarity, as if I have always known them. Perhaps I have.

FALL
3783 B.C.E.

The day after the fall Equinox, several Hechtas visited Devin to discuss Kelan's recent unhappiness. The children's training was scheduled to begin at new moon, and the Hechtas worried that in her present mood, Kelan would disrupt the others and all would fail to learn. She had not played recently with her friends at all, and she ignored Jori in their evenings at home. The Hechtas heard that the Tribeswomen talked about Kelan's attitude, not a good development if Kelan was to be their leader some day.

"Her bitterness affects everyone," Marjika said. "I worry for her."

"I really thought she might adjust," Devin told the assembled Hechtas, "but you are right. She is terribly unhappy."

"Poor thing. We have asked a lot of her," Garnet added. "For weeks now, she has led a party out almost every day."

"I suggest," Petrov's basso voice boomed, "that we take all the children on a special trip so they may play together. Perhaps a few days away will let Kelan enjoy being with her friends again. The Hunters have gathered enough food, grass, and wood to last three winters! The storage houses are all full."

"They have done well," Devin agreed. "I think they gathered every piece of food in walking range! A wall of stacked branches as tall as me surrounds the main hearth, and Daña had enough dried grasses and moss to pile high around every house. To keep out the wind, she even put bales of grass high around the big trenches we dug."

The trenches were for sanitary purposes. Taking care of human waste and other by–products of daily life was not difficult when the Tribe traveled all the time. They just dug a hole for wastes when they arrived at a place and carefully covered it over before they left.

Living year–round in one place required a new system. The trenches sufficed for now, but Devin wanted a better answer, and early on in their new settlement, she thought about the problem, and then put it in the back of her mind. She wanted it to simmer, she told a concerned Daña, until a clear solution emerged. She was sure that in time she would come up with a good plan, but for the present, the trenches would do.

"Kelan deserves a holiday with the other children. They have helped a lot, too, but they have not had to lead," Herta added.

"Well, I could use a walk." Nita was well known in the Tribes for her "walks," as she considered a three–day journey about right just to stretch her legs. "I can take them into the hills to look for zantek roots. They will have a grand time exploring the caves."

"I will join you." Herta loved a walk as much as her friend, and she enjoyed the company of the young ones. "I can look for black stones for marking the hides."

"I will send a messenger to tell Falcone that women and children will be in the hills," Devin told the group.

"Why?" Petrov asked with a defensive tone. "Falcone does not tell us where to go or not go."

"It is just a courtesy. If his people are hunting in the area, the children will scare any animals off," Devin explained.

"I see," Petrov calmed herself.

"I will ask Wren to prepare travel food for a few days," Herta said, unfolding her long frame and leaning over to fit through the doorway.

"We can leave tomorrow," Nita followed her. "Tell everyone who wishes to go to meet at dawn near the garden."

The children were thrilled to go out with Nita, as they enjoyed the big woman's easy ways and sense of fun. Even Kelan smiled, but only after Devin assured her that she had no duties on this trip.

At the next dawn, Nita and Herta met the children near the field as planned. The girls' mothers and other women came as well, all waving as the singing party set out for the hills.

Even Devin hobbled out to see them off. Daña had fixed two long sticks to help Devin walk, carving them flat at the top to be more comfortable under her arms. They held most of Devin's weight, allowing her to move about slowly with little strain on her legs.

The messenger Devin had sent to the men's camp found only the very old and the very young there, which meant a hunting party was indeed out. Devin asked Swain to accompany the children's party to scout for the men and let them know of the children's presence. Swain was happy to go along, and the Scout promised Devin she would smell the scent of the men long before they were anywhere near the children. If men came hunting in the direction of the children's party, Swain promised to alert Nita and steer the children away. Devin had entrusted the Tribe to the Scout's sensitive nose, eyes, and ears many times.

There was another benefit to having the children off on an adventure with the two Hechtas: It gave Devin and Garnet much needed time alone together, and Devin joked to Swain that she intended to make good use of their empty nest over the next few nights. Hearing this, Garnet laughed merrily and said it proved her partner was indeed feeling better.

Whistling, Devin hobbled to Garnet's house.

The steady rise and fall of Swain's chest was not enough movement to scare the fluttering little black bird away from landing on the branch next to her. Had she been hungry, the Scout could have grabbed the bird with her bare hand. She squeaked softly, and the little bird suddenly cocked its head this way and that, then hopped over to the next leafy branch to snatch a bug from a hole in the bark.

Swain's gaze returned to the little hiking group off in the distance as it climbed the first set of hills. They looked like a merry band as they walked happily along. With each gust of the breeze, Swain thought she heard the notes of a song they sang.

She scanned the horizon. A herd of elk ate and walked lazily away from the river, toward the big woods upstream, seemingly unalarmed. Looking to the mountains, her sharp eyes picked out a sprinkling of sheep grazing on hillsides. She saw wispy smoke over the men's camp downstream and wondered if they had already returned from hunting. Astaga had taught Swain that, when she was unsure of what to do, she should stay still, watch, and listen, and if she was patient, the answer would come.

Swain was the best Scout anyone could remember, and she always followed the Toolmaker's advice and Norahjen's wisdom as well. Turning back to the children, Swain saw Jori pick something off the ground and run to Nita for identification.

"It looks like a mountain lion's lost tooth," Nita suggested, returning it to the child. "That is something special."

"Look, Ara!" Jori yelled and ran to catch up with her friend.

Nita smiled at her exuberance. She wished Kelan showed

a little energy, but the sullen child simply walked alongside Herta and said nothing. All the other children spread out, happily scanning the area.

When the sun was high overhead, Nita called for a rest. They had already climbed several hills, and now the ground was craggier with fewer plants and trees breaking the terrain. The party sat in a circle, all chatting and eating the plums that Herta brought along.

"Where are the caves, Nita?" Riala asked. "Will we get there soon?"

Pointing to the slope, Nita answered, "Up there, not too far. When we get to a camping place, our first task is to set out our blankets and gather wood for a fire, then I will show you the caves. Tomorrow, we will look for roots I need."

"And the black stones, too," Herta chimed in.

"Why can we not look today?" asked Jena.

"The Great Bear Mother sleeps in a cave," Herta explained, looking at the girl. "We never enter Her cave after the sun has passed the sky's middle, because that is when She returns from eating and goes to bed. We would disturb Her and Her children. We wait until morning, after She leaves the cave to look for food. If we are careful and do not disturb anything, She does not mind our coming in when She is gone."

As promised, the campsite was not far. Some children gathered firewood while others found stones to ring the firepit that Herta and Nita dug.

"Why do we always put a circle of stones around a fire, Herta?" asked Ana.

Herta, unpacking a sack, saw that five little pairs of eyes watched her. "Does anyone know the answer?" she asked.

No one spoke, so she continued, "We dig a shallow hole to build the fire in, not too deep, and we ring the hole with stones. Both of these things keep the fire from growing too large and running away. Why, this little fire could burn every living thing on this whole mountain if it spread! Have you also noticed we always clear a large area around the fire circle as well? Can you say why, Jori?"

"So the fire has nothing to eat?" Jori suggested as she rubbed her belly in the Hunter's sign for food.

"That is right," Herta smiled at her. "Fire needs to be fed or it dies. The more you feed it, the bigger it grows. Why do the stones keep the fire in the circle, Jena?"

The child looked at the sky and thought hard.

"I know!" Kelan jumped up. "Fire cannot eat stone!"

"Correct, my dear." Herta patted her warmly on the arm, glad to see Kelan join in. "Let us go look at the cave openings, and after that we will eat. Later I will tell you the story of the Great Fire, and you will understand why we are so careful now."

Several caves opened onto a small plateau above the group's camp, and while the area in front of the caves was flat, the ground between their camp and the caves was rocky and steep. There was no easy path, so they climbed over boulders, clinging to small scrub pines that grew between rocks. Once they reached the plateau, they looked over the vista back to their village.

"Oh, my!" Riala exclaimed. "Look how far we came today! I cannot see our home at all!"

"Yes, we came far. Come, children, and see where the cave openings are, but remember, do not enter them today. We will return tomorrow to go inside." Nita motioned the children to follow.

Three caves opened onto the plateau. Two were almost invisible, covered by vines. A good shelter, Jori thought, if you were a Bear or a Hunter caught in a storm. The third was large, its mouth exposed and facing the wind. Nita had the children stand quietly near the opening so they could hear the whistling sounds that the wind made as it blew through rock formations inside.

A rustling in the underbrush startled them all. Little Ara grasped Herta's hand tightly, certain that a Bear had come to eat them all. But only Swain appeared at the far end of the plateau, smiling.

"Ah, Swain," Nita greeted, "what can you tell us?"

"There are no Hunters nearby," Swain reported, "but the Bear Mother and Her three cubs return from the river soon to sleep in their cave here. You should go back to camp and build your fire."

"Will you join us there?" Jori asked excitedly because she loved spending time with the Scout.

"I will, young one," Swain grinned at the child. "A hot meal will taste good, especially one I do not have to cook! I almost had a bird earlier today, but I did not want to make a fire, and I am not as fond of raw fowl as Norahjen."

"Let us go start the fire, then," Nita smiled at the Scout. "I will cook you up something."

In the morning, they broke the fast with cold meat and raisins and drank a hot broth made by Herta. Swain had stayed nearby overnight, but as soon as they finished breakfast, she rose to leave again. Herta and Nita packed a bundle with several empty sacks and some small hand tools, and Nita slung the bundle over her shoulder. They prepared two torches, lit one from the fire's embers, and then climbed the hill again to the plateau.

"Jori and Ara, go with Herta to the big cave. It seems deep enough to contain the stones Herta wants. Kelan, Jena, and Riala, come with me to explore the smaller caves. There are plants under those vines, and we may find the roots we seek," Nita instructed. She took the other torch from Herta and lit it from the first.

At the big cave's entrance, Herta told the girls to wait. She went in a few steps, holding the torch high. The cave was deep and large enough for a woman to stand in a good ways back. She heard water trickling somewhere, but she could not see it. Seeing no live animals or traces of other inhabitants, she motioned the girls inside. They stayed close to Herta and walked toward the sound of water.

Herta grinned when they found the water source. Seepage came from a high crack in the cave wall and pooled on a little shelf at the back. She often found the stones she sought in places just like this.

She pulled two diggers out of her pack and gave them to the girls, demonstrating how to scrape the surface of the soft, wet stone, looking for little black crystals. They found a few and were widening their search when a scream pierced the air like a spear.

Running into daylight, they saw Nita sitting near the edge of the plateau, her shoulder bleeding. Riala and Jena huddled behind her.

Jori ran in front of the woman, instinctively protecting her. Kelan stood in front of Jori, and facing Kelan, not three strides away, was a huge Bear at the plateau's edge.

Herta motioned the girls to be still as she cautiously edged toward the others. As She sniffed and looked intently at Kelan, the Bear pawed at the air, but not in a menacing way.

Kelan's stretched her arm out toward the animal, palm up, and she spoke softly. "Yes, Mother, why are you so upset?" Kelan asked as if she expected the Bear to answer.

Herta kicked a small stone, and the noise made the Bear growl. Kelan said, "NO! Please! Stay there! You scare Her!"

Herta watched helplessly as Kelan stepped toward the Bear. Speaking gently to the huge animal, she reached the roots of a little tree that grew at a precarious angle from the rock's edge. A small cry came from the branches and suddenly Kelan understood: A cub had climbed out too far and was stuck.

"Mother, you are too large to climb this little tree," Kelan continued speaking, "but I am small, and I can go out there and get your child."

The Bear took a small step toward Kelan and grunted a sound that could have been a question, but She did not attack.

Kelan continued, "It is all right, Mother. I will not harm him." She continued her soothing talk as she looked for the best way to climb to the cub. Finding some sturdy branches, she inched her way slowly up and out. The humans held their breath. Herta, watching the Mother Bear, thought She also held Hers.

The little tree bent precariously and some part of it cracked. Startled, the Mother Bear growled and took a step. Kelan reached out, beckoning the cub as she made quiet, coaxing noises. The cub pawed at the girl and suddenly, Kelan grabbed the scruff of his neck and pulled him to her. The frightened baby clung to her shoulder as she climbed carefully down.

When the Mother Bear saw Her cub in Kelan's arms, She moved toward the two. This alarmed Herta and Jori, who both started toward them as well. Kelan froze them in place with a command, "NO! Stay where you are! She only wants Her baby."

Kelan stooped and softly set the little cub on the ground. He wobbled a moment and then hunched over and used all four paws to run to the safety of his mother's shadow. The Great Bear stood up on Her hind legs, head swaying and arms waving through the air. She was only feet away from Kelan, who did not appear frightened at all. Mother Bear bawled and snorted, then looked directly and warmly into the girl's eyes.

Kelan smiled as she bowed her head slightly and said, "Be well, Mother."

The Bear turned from Kelan and ambled down the rocky slope with the cub following behind.

Jori ran to Kelan and hugged her tightly, fighting back tears. "You were so brave!" the young Hunter said.

Herta went to Nita, still bleeding on the ground. The wound was long but, not deep, and it looked like the mark of a Bear claw.

"Let us return to camp," Herta instructed the children.

They picked their way down the slope, Nita leaning on Herta. Kelan built a fire as Herta examined Nita's wound more closely, and then together, they washed and bound the cuts.

Jori walked a few paces away from the camp, cupped her hands over her mouth, and whistled for the Scout who soon came running.

"What happened?" she asked, seeing Nita's shoulder and scanning the others. No one else seemed hurt, but most looked pale and frightened. Riala made a tea for everyone.

"Kelan saved a Bear cub!" Jori blurted to the Scout. "And its Mother clawed Nita!"

"But the Bears are at the river. I was looking right at them when you whistled!" Swain argued, perplexed.

All the children talked at once, and Swain held up her hand for silence.

"All right, tell me the story from the beginning. Nita, please start."

Taking a deep breath, Nita said, "We had gathered roots in one cave and were leaving to go to the other. When we came out, we saw the Bear standing at the edge of the slope, bawling. She came at us on Her hind legs. I stepped in front of the Mother Bear, and She scratched me. I fell down and the Bear leaned over me.

"Kelan spoke to Her as she walked toward the spot where the Bear had stood at first, and the Bear followed. Kelan saw the cub stuck in a small tree that hung over the edge, and she realized that the Mother could not climb out and rescue the cub.

"Kelan kept talking to the Bear, and She made sounds back as if She answered. Then, Kelan climbed the tree and got the cub. The Mother Bear took the cub and left, down the hill." Nita shook her head in amazement at the story she had just told, wondering if she would believe it herself if she had not just seen it with her own eyes.

"Where were you?" Swain asked Herta.

"I was in the big cave with Jori and Ara. We heard the Bear roar and the girls scream, and we came running out. I tried to get between the Bear and the girls, but every time I took a step, the Bear threatened me. Kelan was the only one the Bear allowed to move," Herta said.

"Kelan? What made you take such a risk?" Swain asked.

"I knew Mother Bear was scared so I talked to Her. Then I heard the baby crying in the tree, and I just wanted to help. She meant no harm to us," Kelan said thoughtfully. "I saw it in Her eyes."

"Well, we have to tell this story to the rest of the Hechtas and the Queens," Herta said.

"Yes, let us leave for home as soon as we rest," Swain said, adding a warning, "This is the Bear's territory, and we are trespassing. Because I left the river, I do not know where the rest of the Bears are now."

After tea and a brief rest, the children packed the carrying sacks and Swain led them down the hill. Jori and Ara shared Herta's burden, and Kelan helped Nita over rocky parts.

When they finally reached level ground, Swain sent Jori running to camp for a Healer. Nita insisted she was fine, that it was just a scratch, but Swain sent the child anyway.

That night after the children were tucked in bed, Garnet and Devin sat at the Hechtas' fire.

"So, you tell us that the Bear allowed only Kelan and no one else to get close to the cub?" Marjika asked Herta.

"Yes. I moved toward it but the Bear threatened me. Kelan talked to Her, and I swear the Bear seemed to understand. She made sounds as if She answered. We all watched the Bear Mother choose Kelan to save Her child."

"We might interpret this to mean that the Mother chose Kelan to watch over Her Tribe," Garnet said.

"Do you think this is a sign Kelan should be the next Hearth Queen?" Petrov asked.

"We could interpret it that way," Devin agreed, "and the girl does show a natural talent toward the Hearth Queen's duties."

"She certainly has no taste for hunting," Swain chuckled, "but two times now, she has acted with sense and calm in a crisis. Today she kept her wits and saved the cub, and when Devin and Anna were injured, she took charge until help arrived."

"She is young and needs seasoning, but when the time comes, I will follow her," Nita said to the group.

"As will I," agreed Herta.

"It seems from all accounts that The Mother favors Kelan," Marjika said. "When she chooses her path at Yule, we can all voice our opinions."

"It is not as if she would displace Jori, who so aches to be Hunt Queen," Devin offered.

"True," Garnet agreed, "my daughter shows great promise as a Hunter and builder, but no talent at all for healing or mediation. She would be far happier as Devin's apprentice."

"It will not be easy when the time comes for choosing," Petrov predicted. "The old ones do not like change."

"But we have never shown any difference between the children in our homes. They call us both 'Mama.' They know that Kelan was born of me and Jori of Garnet, but this makes no difference in our daily lives."

"That is so," Marjika commented. "I hear them call you both Mother, regardless of which child speaks to which of you."

"If only they were both recognized as our daughters, there would be no problem," Garnet said thoughtfully, "but we have some time yet. The girls start their training in a few days. Let us keep silent and see what develops."

The first few days of training centered on survival skills. The children learned what to do if they were separated from other members of the Tribe, how to find food and basic medicine plants, where to find shelter, and how to find their way in the wilderness using stars and the sun as guides. Today's lesson was to find medicine and food plants in the wild.

The four girls followed Anna along the edge of the forest upstream of the village. All looked intently at the ground, seeking more of the plants Anna had just shown them.

Hearing voices, everyone looked downstream and saw three men walking to the village. Devin, using just one of her crutches now, walked slowly out to meet them flanked by Tem and Daña.

"Who are those men?" Riala asked.

"The tall one is Falcone," Jori whispered. "They come to speak with Devin about a trade." Jori knew the Queens' plans and spoke with an insider's authority. The girls were impressed.

"What will we trade?" Jena asked.

"We trade some of the extra food we gathered for winter."

"What do we want from them?" Riala asked Anna.

"When spring comes, the men will return to help us gather stones and wood for our buildings. We trade for their work," Anna explained.

As the children watched, Devin patted Falcone on his tall shoulder and they talked while Tem went to find Barde. Devin never led men into the village until Barde sang the Visitor Alert. Anna called the girls back to business.

"So, Falcone," Devin said between sips of tea, "has your hunting been good this summer?"

"Very good, excellent," he answered, his little black eyes shifting constantly back and forth.

He never looks directly at anyone, Devin thought. He is crafty, seeing much more than he seems to, but I must be as diplomatic as I can to get the best trade for the Tribe, she cautioned herself.

"How did you hurt your leg?" Toban inquired graciously.

"Anna slipped on a rock and fell into the water. When I tried to pull her out, I fell in, too."

"It is fortunate you were not hurt worse," Lexis said with concern. "Thank The Mother you are healing well."

"Yes," she nodded.

"And what is this stick that you lean on?" Falcone reached for the crutch.

"Daña made this to help me walk. I had two of them at first, but now I need only one."

"It is simple, but smart," Falcone ran his hands up and down the length of the staff. "You have carved a place where your arm fits. Look, Toban," he said, handing the stick to Toban, who examined it and put it under his own arm.

"Too short to help me, but I see how you did it," he turned a smiling face to the woman who raised him. When Toban was a boy, Devin always said he would keep growing taller until he looked down at her. She smiled, understanding his remark. "I can make one if we need it," Toban added with some of Devin's confidence.

"After you refresh yourselves, I will show you around so you can see the sizes of the buildings that we need stone and wood for," she said amicably.

"Why are your houses so big?" Falcone asked skeptically. "That is not how you have built in the past."

"We are creating new ways," Devin said patiently. "We have never stayed in one place before, and we have to think differently about many things."

"I never change my thinking about anything. I like to stay with what has always worked. It is much safer." His pronouncement surprised no one.

Too bad Shayana is too old for romance, Devin thought wryly. These two are a match of temperament if ever there was one.

"I understand that you built a house for the Healers," Toban tactfully changed the subject. "May I see it?"

Devin smiled, glad the sensible Toban was along. He might become their Healer and not their leader, but the men's Healer advised the leader on many things. He will be a good, steadying influence on his Tribe one day. Devin liked the boy much better than his father, though she could hardly call him a boy anymore.

"I will ask Lia to show you. Perhaps you two can compare skills," Devin smiled at him.

"I would like that," Toban grinned with affection towards Devin. Even though he was grown, Toban had not forgotten how Devin had played with him when he was small and taught him to shoot a bow. Jori was always a better shot, but Devin taught him patiently as well. To this day, he tried to emulate her kindness and patience.

Devin led the men through the village, pointing out the children's house, the Healers' house, the Tribe house, and the storage buildings. At the Healers' house, Devin introduced Toban to Lia and Anna, leaving him there while she continued the tour with just Falcone and Lexis. Tem and Daña followed like silent sentinels.

The party went to the meat house and sat on the wall around the hearth, a fire at the center. Haunches of meat coated with layers of herbs hung over the fire, making the house warm and fragrant. Devin explained how she constructed the smoke hole in the roof and how smoked meat lasted a long time, particularly in cold months, and was tastier than salted or dried meats.

"If we bring you meat next summer, will you show our Cooks how to prepare it this way?" Lexis asked. "We can trade you some of the meat for your labor."

"We will be glad to discuss such a trade next year," Devin agreed. "But now we will give you a haunch of smoked boar for your journey. If you like it, we can talk about a trade next spring."

"You need a lot of stone and wood for these buildings. Do you plan to finish them all in one summer?" Falcone sounded casual as he changed the subject abruptly. Devin knew his question was not.

"Oh, no," Devin smiled, "we will work on the Tribe house first, then the storage houses. I do not know how many we can finish in one season."

"So, you want to trade for enough labor to find, cut, and transport sufficient wood and stones for four, large buildings?" His eyes glinted like the black flint Herta used for arrow tips.

"Yes, I think that is what we need at first," she said cautiously. Now the real negotiations began. She knew Falcone always got the best deal he possibly could for whatever he gave in trade.

"What do you offer us for this service?"

Devin offered the least she could without insulting him, which gave her room to concede something without giving up too much. She knew his respect for her was based partly on her strength in negotiations, as Falcone equated generosity in trades with weakness. She must be strong and unshakable. "We offer one drag of food for each building. That should get you through the winter without hunger."

"We can feed ourselves," he said, sounding testy, but Devin knew one of his trading tactics was to pretend offense at the first offer.

"Of course you can," she reassured, "but we have already done the work, so, in essence, we trade our own work for yours."

"What kind of food . . .?" his voice betrayed only mild interest

She smiled, not fooled by the casual tone. "I offer a total of two drags of grain, one drag of vegetables, and one drag of dried fruits."

"Hmmm . . . let me think a moment," he said, looking out the smoke hole. She was careful not to seem impatient. Falcone stretched the silence, trying to unsettle her. At last he spoke, "I think we need more than that. We want also one drag of kartof and one drag of salt."

"That is too high a price," she said immediately, looking directly at him and making him uncomfortable. She blinked a few times to clear her vision. Maybe it was just the constant movement of his eyes that bothered her. "But we offer one additional drag, half kartof and half salt. Remember, we will see no benefit from this trade until next spring, a long time to wait for payment."

"And you will supply the drags as well?" he asked, his voice innocent.

She clapped him hard on the shoulder. "You are indeed a good trader, my friend," she laughed. "I supply three and you supply two. How is that?"

He grinned, knowing she had seen through his ploy but glad to squeeze one more small concession out of her.

"Done." He grasped both of her shoulders, and she his. They kissed each another on both cheeks to seal the deal.

"When will you come for this food?" she asked.

"When we begin our travel downriver. Today is three days past new moon, and we leave right after the next round if the weather is good. I will send a messenger the day before we depart," he promised.

"Good. I will be sure everything is ready. Will you stay today for a meal? Wren has several birds roasting, and I can talk Marjika out of some wine. You may sleep in the Tribe hut and start out again in the morning."

Lexis looked at him hopefully. "The smell of roast fowl makes me hungry, and I would like to spend time with Marjika as well."

"We stay," Falcone nodded, smiling.

"Good. Perhaps there is a woman of the Tribe you wish to see also, Falcone . . .?" Devin grinned, hoping her comment made it clear that she was not that woman. Falcone was notorious for jumping to his own conclusions at the smallest opportunity, and she was amused by his high opinion of his own attractiveness.

"As a matter of fact, there is. We will visit our friends now." Falcone turned to leave, but at the door he looked back and said, "You have done well here, my friend. Your building is strong and will serve your Tribe well."

"Enjoy your visit," she smiled at him, amazed at his compliment in light of his resistance to change. Perhaps he could appreciate the building because it did not require that he change his own way of life.

"I will tell Toban we stay overnight before I go to Marjika's," Lexis said, heading for the Healers' house.

After the men all left, Devin turned to Tem and Daña, who had not spoken through the entire negotiation. "So? What do you think?"

"You did fine," Tem's voice was flat. Devin looked closely at her friend. Her words did not match her tone of voice, but it was not in Tem's nature to criticize openly the Hunt Queen's decisions.

Daña had no such compunction. "You should not have offered the haunch as a gift. It could have been part of the trade."

"But if they like it, and they will, they will want more next summer. So, it cost us a haunch of boar this year, but I will get much more next summer," Devin explained adamantly.

"You always think ahead," Daña smiled. "Still, I would have given him just the boar instead of three good drags."

"Trust me," Devin grinned. "Come spring, his men will earn the food and will work gladly because they had fuller bellies this winter than in winters past."

"I wonder who he visits?" Daña mused. "Lexis wants to see how Marjika is; she carries his child. But who has shown interest in Falcone?"

"I have no idea," Devin replied. "I think Wren said that Falcone spent time with one of the Cooks' apprentices the last time he was here. But with Falcone, it could be anyone."

"Except Garnet or you," Tem chuckled at her friend.

"True. But we are not alone in our desire to lie only with women."

"Well, I was just curious . . ." Daña murmured.

"If you like him, I can introduce you," Devin offered.

"Yes, by all means. I can ask Lexis to say something if you like," Tem added.

"But . . . I . . ." Daña blushed and stammered. "Oh, Devin!" she scolded, realizing that Tem and Devin were teasing.

"I have to hunt to replace those hides," Tem told her friend.

"Shall I take a party out tomorrow?"

"If you like," Devin said agreeably, "but Jori cannot go. She must attend lessons."

"All right," Tem sounded disappointed. "I will ask Barde to announce that I plan to go out."

"I will go," Daña said with regained composure.

"I need to find Swain, too," Tem mused aloud.

"I can help with that," Devin interjected. "Daña, will you ask Nita for some powder for a signal? She will know what you mean."

Daña nodded and trotted off to the Hechtas' house, returning shortly with a small pouch for Devin. "She said not to use it all. She has to make more and it takes a few days."

Devin threw a handful of the reddish powder into the fire. Immediately, the smoke turned a deep red as it passed through the hole in the roof, then returned to its gray–white color. Devin tossed more powder into the fire, then tucked the pouch into her waistband.

"Swain should come to the village soon."

"Will she be alarmed?" Tem asked.

"No. In an emergency, I use four puffs of red, not two. This signal tells her that I need her, but not because something is wrong," Devin explained.

Daña smiled again, shaking her head. "You are really something!"

"What?" Devin grinned.

"Dogs that cook; houses with fires inside; smoke that sends messages. You are full of 'majik,'" Daña teased.

"'Majik' is wherever you find it, my friend," Devin winked and smiled.

"I am off to seek Barde. I will send my message the regular way," Tem chuckled as she left the house.

"I am off to find my little one," Daña, too, started out the door. "Do you need help to get somewhere?"

"No. I am fine. I will wait for Swain near the hearth. Can you see Nita again for me, though? Ask her to bring wine for our meal and give her this," she said, handing Daña the pouch.

"Of course."

"Thank you," Devin said as Daña left.

"Three guests visit our Tribe. We share a feast at sunset," Barde sang out, walking around the great hearth's new wooden wall. Her rich voice carried far across the encampment. As she approached the Healers' house, Tem beckoned.

"Barde, will you add something to your message for me?" Tem asked.

"Of course, Tem," Barde smiled. "What can I do for my favorite Hunter?"

Tem's smile was warm and her bright eyes glittered merrily. "Let us not speak of what you can really do for me in front of everyone," Tem's voice was low and confidential. "I prefer to save that discussion for a more private time . . ." Tem and Barde shared many loving nights.

Barde laughed, "All right, we will. What message would you like me to deliver to the rest of the Tribe?" she asked, this time more precisely.

"Please tell everyone that I will take a hunting party out in the morning, and anyone who wishes to join should see me," Tem said.

"Certainly, love. May we discuss your more private requests after the feast tonight?"

"We may," Tem grinned. "I will come to your house."

"Excellent!" Barde squeezed her hand and continued her way through the village with her announcements.

Tem smiled and watched her lover walk away.

"This roasted fowl is most excellent!" Falcone complimented Wren at the meal. "How do you get the meat so . . . tender?"

"We cook it slowly." Wren loathed this man. She could not put her finger on the reason, but she felt angry inside whenever he spoke to her. Of course, no one could see this reaction in her outward demeanor.

"I will tell my Fire Keepers not to be in such a hurry, then, if this is the result," he laughed. "I was told that a child here faced down a Bear. Who was it?"

Falcone scanned the table and looked expectantly at Jori, but it was Kelan who spoke.

"I did not face Her down, exactly," Kelan said haltingly. Falcone looked at the girl, startled.

"You?!? How did this happen?"

"The Mother Bear's cub was stuck in a tree, Falcone, and Kelan climbed out to rescue him," Garnet said proudly.

"Come, sit, and tell me the story, child," he said, patting the bench.

Kelan smiled, happy for his attention. She sat at Falcone's side and told the tale. When she finished, he patted her shoulder. "You were very brave, Kelan, very brave indeed."

Garnet watched the exchange intently, amazed at how gentle Falcone could be with children, especially when she remembered how harshly he barked at his Hunters. Perhaps he is like a crystal, she thought, with many sides.

"Will she take your place, Garnet? After all, you revere the Bear Mother, and She seems to have chosen this one." He threw his arm around Kelan, who sat up straighter.

"Her path will be determined after Yule," Garnet replied, "as is our custom."

"She cannot be Hearth Queen!" came a strident voice from the other end of the table. "She is Devin's daughter, not yours!"

Garnet sighed. She did not wish to debate Alecia right now.

"But the girls were raised as sisters by you both, were they not?" Falcone asked Garnet, puzzled.

"Yes, they were, and I consider Kelan as much my daughter as Jori is," Garnet said staunchly. How ironic that Falcone understands this even though he visits only a few times a year, but Alecia does not, she thought.

"But she was NOT born of your body!" Alecia said stubbornly.

"Alecia, please, this is not the time for this discussion. We will argue these points at the Winter Council, not now when we are entertaining guests." Her icy tone left no room for reply.

Alecia stormed off. Garnet looked ruefully at Devin, glad that the Healers had kept Shayana away from this table or the scene would have been worse. Women would talk about this nonstop now that Falcone had unwittingly brought it up.

Falcone talked quietly to Kelan, who nodded and smiled. He is a good friend, Garnet thought. He stood up for Kelan and now comforts her. She awarded him a smile and asked, "How much longer will you stay in the mountains, Falcone?"

"I think we start downstream near the next round. I will send a messenger the day before we leave so Devin can prepare our trade goods."

"Falcone, did you hear that Jori made her first kill this summer?" Devin asked, wanting to include Jori in her father's attentions.

"I did not!" he sounded impressed. "So, young Jori, do you like to hunt?"

"I do, Falcone!" Jori looked into his eyes. "I have my own bow and quiver of arrows."

"How did you come to make a kill at your young age?" he asked. "Was it a rabbit or a fowl?"

"It was an elk," she said proudly.

"An elk!?!" he exclaimed. "Well, now! That IS impressive!"

"It was a young buck," Jori conceded, remembering to be modest, "with just small horns. He came along the tree line where we hid, and when he saw me, he stopped to look."

"You shot before he had a chance to run away!" he smiled approvingly.

"Jori reacted so quickly," Kelan bragged on her sister's prowess, "that I felt dizzy. The elk was standing right there, and then all of a sudden he was on the ground before I even blinked."

"That is excellent, Jori!" he beamed with pride at his daughter, and Jori grinned right back.

The rest of the evening passed merrily. When all had eaten, Nita brought out a jug of wine and the drummers performed.

"Where is Barde?" Garnet asked her partner quietly.

"I saw her leave with Tem," Devin grinned slyly.

"No songs for us tonight, eh?" Garnet teased, glad that her friends took time with one another.

"Nan will sing, dear," Devin reassured. "See? Here she comes now." Nan was Barde's young apprentice. She went directly to Petrov and spoke quietly, then, with a little bow, took her place among the musicians.

By the rounding of the moon, the children had settled into the routine of daily instructions. After breakfast, lessons were first thing in the morning. The girls rested after lessons, then took a snack from the hearth and were assigned chores for the afternoon. But today they were excused from chores.

Today, Falcone's Tribe was leaving the area, and most of the Tribeswomen walked downstream behind drags of trading goods to see their friends off. Everyone helped pull the drags except the smallest children and Devin, who now walked without the crutches but still followed the Healers' advice to take only easy walks.

The messenger had arrived the day before and asked Devin to prepare the trade goods and meet the men at a particular spot. Devin messaged back her agreement and alerted Barde.

Ara bounced along beside Jori, skipping her happiness at being in her older friend's company. Since Jori began training, they had much less time together.

"Why does Falcone's Tribe leave?" Ara wanted to know.

"To travel with the herds as they always do. Lexis said he did not want to stay always in one place as we do now," Jori answered.

"We do not stay here always. We go on hunts and walks," Ara's young mind worked logically.

"But we always return to this village."

A commotion rose at the front of the group as women saw the first men coming down the trail, waving and smiling. Jori saw Toban beside their father and followed her mother to approach them.

"Hello," Garnet smiled, embracing Falcone and Toban. "We have brought the trade items as promised and some gifts."

She gave a fine fur robe to Toban and a soft hide to Falcone. Both thanked her profusely.

"We brought you a gift, too," Falcone said, pointing to the drag full of fish that one of the men pulled near. "Lexis thinks that these might taste good smoked as you did the boar."

"That they would, I think," Devin smiled. "When you return, we will give you some."

"We brought a jug of goat's milk in hopes your cooks would make some of their wonderful cheese," Toban said, indicating a large jug on the second drag.

"How do you get goats to give you milk?" Jori wondered aloud. Jori did not know the men's way with goats because her Tribe did not often use milk from animals, except to make cheese when the men's Tribe provided the raw milk. The women's Tribe thought of milk as The Mother's gift to each animal's babies, and they feared that if they took the mother's milk, baby animals would starve.

The men claimed they had a special bond with the goats and were allowed to take their milk at certain times of the year. The men and boys even drank goat's milk from cups, and they brought it as a gift and to trade when they visited the women. Many seasons ago a Hearth Queen had learned how to make cheese from milk from one of the sister tribes in the desert, and Garnet's Tribe had made goat's milk cheese this way since she was a child.

Toban smiled at Jori to answer her question, "It takes two of us to get milk from one goat: One holds the goat and the other pulls its teats to squeeze the milk out."

"How many goats do you have to milk to get that much?" she asked, looking at the big jar, half as tall as she.

"As many as I have fingers," Toban held up his hand, grinning. "We milked all afternoon yesterday."

"Wren will be happy to make cheese," Garnet said, smiling.

Many women and men brought gifts for one another. Lexis stood with Marjika a little ways away from the crowd.

"I made this for the coming child," he smiled gently, handing her a small sack about as long as her arm from the elbow down. Its outside was a soft, brown hide and there was a drawing at the top; the inside was lined with soft, dappled brown and white rabbit fur. "For you to carry her around after she is born."

Marjika kissed him. "It is beautiful. Did you draw the animals?"

"Yes, and it took me a long time!" he laughed at himself. "I fear drawing is not my best skill."

"I like it," she said, "and if the child is male, I will be happy for you to raise him."

Falcone's voice called the men to begin their journey.

Lexis hugged her tightly. "Merry part, Marjika. Be well."

She looked deeply into his eyes. "Merry part, Lexis. Return soon."

The women watched Falcone's Tribe take its first of many steps downriver, waving and shouting goodbyes until the men were but tiny figures. Devin nudged Garnet and nodded at Marjika, standing close to Lia.

The Healer whispered to Marjika, who put her head on Lia's shoulder as they walked back to the village. Garnet smiled at Devin, happy at the thought of Lia becoming involved with someone. She had been lonely so long, and it would certainly help erase her feelings for Garnet.

"Nita or Herta can help the children make their masks," Lia said. "You must rest now. This has been a long walk for you."

"I am still fit enough to walk twice this distance without resting!" Marjika protested.

"But the young one you carry is not," Lia scolded gently.

Marjika finally consented to a short rest while Herta and Lia helped the children make animal masks for the coming Harvest Day Festival. On Festival Day, children wore masks of animals they felt especially close to or even looked or acted like in some ways. The Tribe honored the children's animal spirits with small gifts of fruit or sweets and celebrated its harvest bounty with a mouth–watering feast.

Astaga taught children the two purposes of the Harvest Day Festival: the first, to celebrate a summer of good hunting and reward the Tribeswomen for their hard work; the second, to honor and thank both animal and human ancestors for their bounty. The Tribeswomen thanked animal ancestors for gifts of meat, fur, hide, and tools, and they thanked their human ancestors for the gift of knowledge–handed–down on which the Tribe's very survival depended.

The Tribe's Elders represented the human ancestors, and they were pampered the entire day of the Festival. Women bathed them, anointed them with sweet oils, dressed them in beautiful, new clothes made specially for the occasion, and served their meals before anyone else.

In conjunction with the Harvest Festival, the children's classes these days focused on the turning of the seasons, the four major festivals of the year, and other smaller rituals that corresponded with the passage of time.

At the moment, though, the children were absorbed in the project at hand, making masks for Festival Day. Jori wanted to become a great feline and was tying bushy, dried stalks together to make a tail. Astaga suggested that Kelan represent the Great Bear Mother, and the girl carved a mask from a slab of bark. Riala used feathers to decorate a bark–mask of a bird, and Jena worked on a reindeer mask with antlers.

"Oh, I hope that Wren makes sticky cakes this year!" Jena said excitedly.

"She has not missed as far back as I can remember, except for that year we had no raisins. She used plums and the cakes were not really sticky."

"I like the dried apple slices," Riala smiled.

"I like the games," Jori put in. "Last Harvest, I won a race!"

Preparations for the feast were underway throughout the village. Devin organized her first hunting trip since her injury. Garnet planned the ritual ceremony with Nita in the Temple. Petrov worked with musicians, cleaning and repairing instruments. Barde rehearsed a group of women to sing the Harvest Song. The Festival was just a few days off, at the dark of the moon.

"The elk grow their winter coats already," Tem observed.

"So Swain said," Devin replied. "I hope we can get a few. That first growth is so soft and can be made into good baby gifts. The Hechtas want to make welcoming presents for the two new ones."

"When will the children come? Have the Healers said?"

"Anna says right after Yule, so if we get the soft hides now, there will be plenty of time to make blankets."

"Barde will sing your announcement today and tomorrow. We go the next morning?"

"Yes. That leaves us one day before the Festival to prepare the meat. I hope many women want to go." The Harvest Festival's hunt usually attracted more women than a regular hunt. "I probably need both you and Daña to help organize everything and everyone."

"I am sure Daña will not mind helping," Tem nodded. "She does not hunt often in summer, but she loves hunting in the fall and winter."

"I will speak to her today."

"Is your leg ready for this?" Tem's concern sounded in her tone.

"Anna says it is fine. I have been out walking good distances, and it has not tired or ached from climbing," Devin reported, "so stop mothering me. I know what I am doing."

Tem grunted, "Right."

"What?"

"You speak to ME now," Tem tapped her own chest with her fingertips. "I am Tem, your friend since childhood. I know how you push yourself."

"I am fine, really. Do not worry, my friend. Anna said I could go."

"Well, I do trust Anna's assessment. She is not nearly as

stubborn as you," Tem teased, "and Daña and I will be along to keep an eye on you."

Many Tribeswomen hunted only in the spring and in the fall. Other duties kept them busy the rest of the year, but the Harvest hunt and the first hunt of spring were important to the life of the Tribe so everyone pitched in. Most of the time, Devin led only a handful of Hunters; this time about 20 women would make the trek.

"Always sharpen the point in the same direction," the Tool–maker counseled Jori and Ara. "Start at the shaft, here, then slide the stone away from yourself, all the way past the tip. Give a little flick with your wrist as you come off the point." She demonstrated the sharpening technique, then watched the girls concentrate as they practiced. "You two work on these arrows. Take your time with them. Pile the sharp ones here, and I will come back to check."

Astaga had been busy making and sharpening arrows and spears for several days now, and the increased work just before a big hunt irritated her. She believed women should make sure their arrows and spears were always sharp and ready to use, and she considered it lax that so many women ignored their weapons until right before a big hunt. The full–time Hunters never did such a thing, but even those who only hunted twice a year should keep their weapons in good working order, Astaga thought. What if there was trouble? She sighed loudly.

She had asked their mothers if Jori and Ara could help in the afternoons after their lessons. These two were good helpers, and with her regular apprentice as well, she supposed the work would get done.

Jori and Ara felt extraordinarily lucky at this turn of events. They both loved to spend time with the Hechtas, and both were also allowed to go on the hunt. As it turned out, all the children were going, as were their mothers. Jori and Ara paid close attention to their duties; Astaga was a good teacher and they wanted to please her.

On the day of the hunt, Devin, Tem, Daña, and Jori met Swain at the edge of the village in the chilly, half–light of morning. Jori saw her breath as she stood behind Devin and listened to the adults plan.

Swain reported a good–size herd of reindeer was in the low hills. This herd did not go to the river each morning as others did. They stayed in the hills, drinking from springs and runoffs on craggy slopes and eating leafy vines that hung from boulders and trees.

The leaders decided to hunt this herd instead of looking for elk near the river. Once the rest of the women and children assembled, Swain ran off to the hills. Devin addressed the crowd.

"We walk to the second layer of hills," Devin spoke loudly enough for all to hear. "The Scout has seen reindeer up there. We will wait at the base of the second hills until Swain comes to take us to the herd. After Swain arrives, stay silent until the signal is given. Look to Tem and Daña if you cannot see me."

Standing in the rear of the crowd with Ara, Jori felt a tug on her quiver and turned to see Astaga walking away. Ara pointed at Jori's quiver, and Jori looked over her shoulder. Her heart leapt as she saw three new arrows among those she herself had made! She checked Ara's quiver and saw that she, too, had been rewarded for her labor. Ara's face shone with joy.

The sun was directly overhead when they reached the base of the second set of hills. Devin signaled them to rest, and everyone sat down, some munching on fruit or other snacks.

Kelan and Riala sat near Garnet, both happy that she had come along. Some Hearth Queens did not go on big hunts, preferring to stay in camp and prepare for ritual, but Garnet was a good Hunter and she enjoyed this time with the other women, so she always came. She was especially glad to spend this time with her Tribeswomen since she had missed the Summer Gathering. Looking across the slope at Devin, she remembered acutely how she had missed her partner last summer! She was glad to be with the hunting party rather than waiting for their return in the village.

Devin inspected one of the arrows Jori had made and nodded approvingly as she ran her finger along the feathered end. She sighted down the shaft and found it was true. Smiling at Jori and patting her shoulder, Devin handed the arrow to Tem, who repeated the inspection and nodded her satisfaction.

Devin silently held her hand out to Ara, who dutifully pulled an arrow from her little quiver and gave it to the leader. Both women inspected the younger girl's arrows equally closely and smiled their approval.

Garnet was amused at the scene. The Hunters wore serious faces and did not give any hint that this inspection was less serious than if the girls were grown–up Hunters facing review by Astaga herself. Garnet loved the Hunters for this. The girls were proud of their work, and the Hunters' acknowledgement helped them feel connected to the whole. As Jori and Ara trotted off, Devin and Tem exchanged smiles.

"Your mother inspected our first arrows, too, remember?" Tem asked.

"I do, and my work back then was not nearly as good as Jori's is today. Did you see that feathering? It looked like your fine work! I could barely tell Jori's arrows from the ones Astaga made."

"It is good to see them hunting together," Tem smiled. "They are much like us."

"They are indeed," Devin clapped her friend on the back. "I hope their friendship is strong like ours when they grow up."

Swain arrived with news of the herd. The leaders spread the

Hunters out in a long line, and the group crept to just below the crest of the hill and looked over. They saw the reindeer herd at the bottom of the next slope.

Devin crouched in the middle of the long line and sent Daña and Tem in each direction at a trot, carrying instructions and checking the women's readiness. Both returned to Devin and signaled all was ready.

Devin closed her eyes and breathed deeply to center herself. All the women and children were quiet but ready.

At the signal, Hunters crept down the hill to get closer to their targets. Jori spotted one small animal off to the right, nibbling on vines that hung down a rock wall. She tapped Ara and headed for this one.

Devin gave the signal to fire, and Hunters rushed toward their prey with an explosion of noises. Women ran and fired; reindeer jerked their heads up, startled, and ran away.

Both Jori and Ara got shots off at their target as the animal turned to run. Jori's arrow hit the reindeer in the flank, and the wounded animal ran across the slope away from the main group of Hunters.

"I must chase it," she called to Ara, "so it does not die slowly. Stay here and wait for the others," Jori shouted over her shoulder as she ran after the reindeer.

Ara walked to the wall to retrieve her arrow. As she bent to pick it up, she saw an opening in the rocks. A cave! I could be the first to discover it, she thought. She entered the cave's darkness and looked around as her eyes adjusted. She had to feel along the wall to find her way toward the back.

Suddenly, Ara heard a deep, rumbling growl and froze on the spot. The Bear had been sleeping and was not happy to be awakened. It stood and towered over the terrified girl.

Ara backed slowly to the wall. She felt a little crevice about as high as her shoulder and quickly squeezed into it. She notched her arrow and held her bow ready, but she did not plan to shoot the Bear unless it came too close. "HELP ME!" she called.

Garnet sensed, rather than heard, the child's cry. She froze, listened until the sound came to her clearly, and ran toward it. She slowed when she saw the cave opening. She heard the Bear bawl and Ara cry out again, and she ran to the entrance, yelling to distract the Bear.

The Bear came as far as the cave opening and stood on its hind legs, sniffing at the newest intruder.

Garnet spoke softly and approached the animal. When she got too close, the Bear pawed at her and Garnet backed away.

She called to the child, "Do not move, Ara! Make no sound! Just stay where you are, and make yourself as small as you can."

Several Hunters heard the commotion, ran up, and stopped to stand at the ready around the cave entrance. Some held their bows ready to shoot. The Bear stood menacingly in the cave's entrance, swatting at anyone who came too close. The circle of Hunters tightened.

"Wait!" Kelan yelled, running to the Hunters. "Do not kill Her! That is a Bear Mother!"

The Hunters parted to let the child through. She went to Garnet. "That is the Bear we saw. The tree Her cub was stuck in is right over there!" the girl pointed down the slope. "Let me talk to Her. She let me come close before."

"No, Kelan. The Bear will kill you AND Ara," Garnet warned.

"She will not!" Kelan said stubbornly and walked right over to the entrance before Garnet could stop her.

Kelan stopped and spoke softly to the Bear. "Mother, you remember me, do you not? I helped your baby. Now I ask you to let me help my friend." She walked slowly into the dark cave. The Bear watched her, paws down, making short, moaning noises.

A moment later, Ara emerged, followed by Kelan, who backed out of the cave facing the Bear and talking still. "Thank you, Mother, for saving this child. We revere your strength." Kelan bowed to Her.

As soon as they were clear of the entrance, Garnet grabbed both girls and walked quickly away from the cave, holding them close. The Hunters backed away cautiously. After they were a good distance from the cave and the Bear, Garnet put the children down.

"Kelan," she admonished, "that Bear could have killed you!"

"She would not," Kelan said indignantly. "She remembered me. I could tell."

"What happened?" Devin came running breathlessly.

"A Bear trapped Ara in Her cave!" one of the Hunters said. "She would not let Garnet near, but Kelan walked right in and brought Ara out!"

"Is everyone all right?" Devin asked.

"No one was hurt," Garnet assured her.

"The Mother Bear chose Kelan again to care for the children," Nita observed. Garnet looked at Nita, wondering when she had arrived. "I think it is a sign," Nita added.

"Let us take the reindeer meat back to the village right now," Devin instructed everyone.

"Devin, may I first leave a gift of thanks for the Bear Mother?" Jori said, pointing to her own kill that she had dragged from the brush.

"A good idea," Devin said. "Let us take it to the cave entrance."

They dragged the little reindeer within a few arms' lengths of the cave. "Mother, we honor you and offer you this food. We give thanks for your wisdom and abundance," Jori said loudly as they backed away from the now-silent cave.

The women cleaned and dressed their kill of four reindeer and hauled them to the village. Their talk on the way was not of the successful hunt, but of Kelan's feat. Kelan and the Mother Bear had now met twice, and both times the Bear favored Kelan over an adult.

They arrived home in the dark. After ritual greetings, they delivered the meat to the Cooks and the horns and hooves to the Hechtas before everyone went to their rest.

Savory smells woke Kelan on the morning of the Harvest Day Feast. It was just past dawn and already roasting was well underway. Kelan washed her face and hands and reported to Wren to learn her duties. The children had been told to help the Cooks in the morning, after which they could don their masks and play all afternoon.

"You can help make the sweets," Wren promised the child, smiling. Kelan hugged Wren excitedly. Helping the apprentices was her favorite assignment!

Kelan walked to the apprentices' area, where the young women told her to dip little balls of flatbread dough into a sticky mixture, then put each on a big green leaf. Kelan did not usually like getting her hands dirty, but she did not mind when it was in the service of sticky confections! Another apprentice folded the leaf into a packet and placed the packets at the base of the fire. Still another watched and occasionally turned the packets until the dough was baked, then took them to a table for unwrapping.

As she dipped the dough–balls, Kelan saw other children coming and going in pairs, hauling jugs of water from the river. She was glad she was spared that backbreaking work, even if her own assignment kept her longer at the hearth.

When she was finally released, Kelan went home to find that Devin had laid out her costume, and she whispered thanks to her mother for the courtesy. Kelan knew that both her mothers had substantial duties on Feast days and little time for themselves, so Devin's kindness was especially thoughtful.

Her deep brown robe was made of elk hide and darkened with berry juice. She pulled it over her shoulders and tied it shut at the collar. She lifted the Bear mask over her face, adjusting the eyes so she could see where she walked. Fully disguised, she went in search of other animal–children.

"There you are!" Riala ran up to Kelan. "You had to work a long time today!"

"Not as long as our mothers," Kelan replied with as much dignity as her Bear outfit allowed. "Besides, I got to dip the sticky breads."

"So what?" Jori teased her. "We have been eating them while you worked on them!"

Jori displayed two of the confections and handed one to her sister. "Here, have one. We had an early start."

"I know!" Jena yelled, "Let us go to the Healers' house!"

The children scampered through the village to the Healers' and began their pantomime. They crawled and ambled around the door, making animal noises that matched their disguises until Anna emerged, grinning.

"What is this? Am I beset by spirits?" she laughed. "Well, I will just have to offer gifts to keep the animal spirits happy!"

She gave each child an apple. "Here you are. Enjoy them. I had no easy time climbing that tree!" The children ran off shouting happily.

Everyone was not as exuberant as the children, however. Outside the Hechtas' house, Shayana was having a fit as Lia tried to bathe and oil her. She had continued to lose her wits through the fall, and now she did not seem to grasp her surroundings or what was happening at all.

"It is Harvest Day, Mother!" Lia said loudly but gently. "I am trying to make you comfortable."

Maybe it was because the Healers or one of their apprentices attended Shayana every day, maybe it was because Shayana had never really liked Lia, or perhaps she was just confused. For whatever reason the old woman was by turns terrified and blustering with anger.

"You do not bathe me!" Shayana yelled. "And why are we here? I have my own house!"

Anna came up quickly.

"Do you need me?" she asked Lia.

"Thank you, love. She will not sit still for me. She is upset and understands nothing, but she has been shouting for you."

Anna approached Shayana as she would a frightened child.

"There, there, dear. It is Anna. You are fine," she cooed.

Shayana calmed enough so that Lia could bathe and dress her, but she did not allow Anna to leave her sight.

Swain watched with great amusement as she sat on a stump in front of the Temple and told Herta about the incident with the Bear.

"You are certain it is the same Bear?" Herta asked the Scout.

"Yes, the same Bear, the same cave. Bears stay in one cave many years, you know. I did not see the cubs; they may have been inside the cave, too. No one got inside except Kelan, and she said it was too dark to see anything."

"Did the Bear take the offering?" Herta asked.

"Oh, yes. She ate the meat, all right," Swain grinned.

"I would like to have the antlers and hooves for Kelan," Herta said. "Do you think you could retrieve them after the Bear is done?"

"I can go in the afternoon when they are away," Swain

offered. "They fatten themselves for the winter now, and they go to the river most days. But the animal was Jori's kill, was it not?"

"Yes, and Jori was wise to offer the animal to the Mother," Herta nodded. "That is all the more reason to give Kelan the tools I make from the kill."

"I will bring them as soon as I can," Swain promised.

"Perhaps I can assist you," a melodious voice offered.

Startled, both women turned.

"You are the only one who can sneak up on me!" Swain laughed, jumping to her feet and hugging Norahjen.

"I did not sneak," Norahjen countered, thumping her apprentice on the back enthusiastically, "I simply approached from an unexpected direction."

"Why did you circle the village and come from upstream? Were you trying to fool me?"

"I just wanted to see the whole thing," Norahjen told her. "It is a beautiful village! Hello, Astaga."

"Hello, old friend," Astaga greeted her. "Are you home for the winter?"

"I am."

"May I brew some tea for you?" the Toolmaker offered.

"Perhaps in a while. First, I will let Devin and Garnet know I am here."

FALL
1984 C.E.

Through the fall, I helped Aranna gather and preserve fruits, nuts, vegetables, and meat. She taught me to smoke hams and fish by hanging them in a small, round building with a fire in the center. She taught me to make jellies and jams from fruits that grew on trees near her cabin.

She talked about the time when the men's and women's Tribes still lived apart. The men's Tribe visited periodically to trade or socialize. Some women had ongoing relationships with certain men; others shared time with various people, men and/or women, depending on their moods. She said some women avoided men and had relationships only with other women. I asked how their society handled all that.

"Handled?" she had said, surprised. "Why would they have to handle anything?"

"Were these practices accepted?" I asked.

"The Tribe's most sacred belief is individual choice," her tone implied that I was too slow to understand this most obvious and basic fact. "Who someone shares pleasure with is a most personal matter. If one woman prefers to eat elk and another prefers rabbit, do others get to accept or reject her desires?"

I had to smile. Aranna had lived in these woods all her life, and for the past decade she had lived alone. Before that, she lived with other surviving members of her Tribe. She had never seen a city. She saw airplanes only as they flew high overhead. She had no idea about the poisons that gripped the world, and I envied her.

During the times that Aranna told me about, the Tribe had no running water, no wheeled vehicles or wagons, and few domesticated animals, yet they seemed a far more civilized people than any society now on the planet. They had education, trade, respect for others, and they were developing agriculture and the arts. They handled conflicts within the Tribe with discussion and mediation. I wanted to time–travel back and stay with them.

WINTER
3783 B.C.E.

"**D**o not step on the ice until you test its depth with a spear," Tem warned the children. "The ice here does not usually freeze thick enough to walk on because the river's water moves all the time. There are places in the high meadows where water stands still, and the ice freezes thicker there. Before you step on ice, it should be as thick as the distance from the tip of your finger to your wrist," she said, extending her finger to indicate the measurement.

Tem taught the lessons today. Tired of being indoors, the children had been restless the past few days, so Tem volunteered to take them to the river. Just a few days of lessons remained before Yule, when they would be excused from lessons for a time because at Yule, decisions would be made about the girls' futures.

"What if I see a fish under there? Can I grab it?" Jori wanted to know.

"Well," Tem looked thoughtful, "you could do that if you had to. Of course, the water is VERY cold for human hands and feet, and no part of you should be in water that is this cold for longer than three breaths. Even after that, you must make sure your wet parts are warmed and dried right away."

"Why?" Ara asked, kicking at the chunky ice that lined the edge of the river.

"Because icy water can give you the white skin," Tem warned. "The Healers say body parts that turn white from cold may never be useful again."

"Anna says you can get the hot–head disease from getting wet in the winter if you do not get warm right away, too," Kelan offered.

"Yes, that is one idea," Tem acknowledged. "In any case, try not to get wet when it is so cold. This is one more reason we smoked all that fish this fall. Now we do not need to fish all winter long."

"But this is not so every winter, is it?" Jena remembered a winter with little stored food when she was smaller.

"No, Jena," Tem answered, "some years we have much less food, and then we fish and hunt whenever we can. We used to travel in winter to the sea where it is warmer, but even there sometimes, the winter food supply was lean."

"What if we have to fish?" Jori persisted.

"Well, I rub fat on my hands and feet to protect my skin, and I wear my big boots. I still fish fast and get right back to the hearth to warm myself as quickly as I can."

"But you said . . ." Riala began

"I said that fishing in ice water involves risk, but sometimes the need is greater than risk. I am a Hunter. I do my duty to the Tribe. Now, let us walk to the edge of the trees, and I will show you where a reindeer found food under the snow."

The snow was as deep as Tem's knees, and she walked ahead so the children could follow in the path she cleared.

"HEY!" Jori yelled when a snowball hit her in the back. She saw Ara packing more snow and quickly joined her friend. The two girls laughed and threw snowballs at other children who threw their own right back. Tem watched all the children join in, some even brave enough to throw a snowball at her. Grinning now, she said, "All right, you lot. Keep going. We need to all get home and warm soon."

As they reached the edge of the woods, Tem walked along the tree line until she saw what she sought. Drawing the children near, she pointed to the ground where snow had recently been disturbed. The children saw large hoof tracks.

"These are reindeer tracks, and this," Tem said, wiping away snow to uncover small, green shoots, "is what she was looking for. Here, try one." She pulled some shoots up and passed one to each child who made faces as they bit into them.

"These taste bitter when raw, but you can eat them if you have no other food. Of course, they taste better when Wren cooks them. Now, let us return to the village to get warm and dry," Tem instructed. "We have been out in the cold long enough."

From their vantage point in front of the Temple, Astaga and Norahjen watched the children follow Tem back to the village's center hearth.

"I hope the children enjoyed being outside for a while," the Toolmaker commented.

"Yes," the Scout agreed, "they have been working hard at their lessons."

Astaga and Norahjen sharpened stone knives that Wren had brought the Toolmaker the day before.

"The day for the Council arrives soon."

"You sound worried, old friend," Norahjen looked at Astaga.

"I am. So are the Queens," Astaga stopped stroking the blade.

"Are their daughters' choices not clear?"

"What the girls want is not the issue," Astaga explained.

Norahjen squinted, "Then, what?"

"The Elders believe Kelan must be Hunt Queen."

"Kelan? Hunt Queen?" The Scout was astounded. "What of Jori?"

"They believe she must be Hearth Queen."

"Preposterous!" Norahjen shook her head. "That is ridiculous. A blind woman can see that it must be the other way."

"Some speak of tradition, believing the Queens' daughters should follow the paths of their mothers, as daughters have always done. Shayana is especially stubborn on this point."

"But the girls do follow their mothers' paths!" Norahjen insisted.

"Not the paths of their mothers by birth."

"I will speak with Shayana myself," Norahjen muttered, rising.

"NO!" Astaga held up a warning hand. "If you do, she will grow even more stubborn and listen to no one. You know how she feels about your opinion of anything."

Norahjen sat back down with a sigh. "I suppose you are right, but these girls' choices cannot be denied."

"Wait for the Council. You will persuade more people by being calm and thoughtful," Astaga suggested.

"All the Hechtas intend to speak on the girls' behalf. Together we will find a way to make it right."

"I need to go walking to clear my head. I am so angry, I do not trust myself to remain silent until Council. I will return when I calm down." The Scout unfolded her huge frame and strode off to pack for a long hike in the hills.

Astaga returned to her sharpening and thought that she had not seen Norahjen this angry in many seasons. The old Scout usually radiated serene calm and became riled only rarely. But Norahjen's emotions ran deep, like still water, and when her temper flared it sometimes boiled over. Astaga pitied the person who confronted the Scout before she regained her balance.

Children scampered into the Tribe house. The big building had become the social center of the village, replacing the large, outdoor hearth as the main daily gathering place. A fire blazed warmly in the central hearth and pots of tea sat on surrounding walls, staying warm or steeping. Women sat in small groups, some sewing hides into clothing, some carving wood or stone, some talking. Two Cooks tended the fire.

Jena ran to a woman playing with Ara and little Marianna; Kelan followed closely.

Jori left Riala sitting on the hearth's low wall to go talk to Devin, who was scratching a drawing into the dirt with a stick. Swain pointed to a spot on the drawing as other Hunters looked on.

"May I go help Astaga?" the child asked excitedly. "She is sharpening knives, and she said I could help her if I had your permission as well."

Devin looked at the others, knowing they all shared the same thought. With no fanfare, she pulled a leather sheath from her waistband and handed it to Jori. She wanted to show her trust in the girl by letting Jori sharpen her own knife, and she fervently hoped that Herta had taught the girl well.

"Here," she said matter of factly to Jori, "you may practice on my belt knife."

One by one, each Hunter followed Devin's lead and handed her knife to Jori. Devin looked at the ground to hide proud tears. No matter what happened in Council, this moment confirmed Jori's future leadership of the Hunters, as they would never give their tools to a mere child. Along with their bows, arrows, and spears, the Hunters' knives were critical to the Tribe's survival. Devin and the other Hunters now entrusted that survival to Jori.

Jori took each sheath solemnly. "I will not fail you," she said quietly and left the house.

As always, Astaga was glad to see the girl. She enjoyed Jori's sharp mind and deft hands, and the Toolmaker took pleasure in teaching her many useful skills. Jori caught on quickly and always asked challenging questions. Astaga believed this was the mark of the girl's true self: She always searched for ways to improve what was, always questioned. She reminded Astaga of Devin at the same age.

Like all Hunt Queens before her, Devin was apprenticed to each Hechta before she spent several seasons as apprentice to her mother. The next Hunt Queen would do the same.

Astaga believed that the next Hunt Queen was the girl who now walked carefully toward her, carrying Hunters' knives. Astaga had never spent much time with Kelan, even though the child was the next Hunt Queen by birth. Kelan could learn the tasks and would do her duty conscientiously, but Jori was the one who truly loved the skills of the Hunt Queen. That Kelan was destined for other, equally important things, Astaga was certain.

"What have we here?" she watched Jori carefully place the knives on the ground and sit on a stump.

"When I asked for permission to help you sharpen tools, Devin gave me her knife to sharpen as well. Then the other three Hunters standing there did the same thing," Jori looked at the Toolmaker to see what she thought of this.

Astaga kept her reactions to herself. "Well, well. Will you start with your mother's knife, then?"

Jori pulled Devin's long blade from the hide sheath. It was heavy, made of metal. Devin had traded for it years ago at the Gathering, attracted to the Bear that was carved into the white stone handle.

While they worked, Astaga told stories about the Tribe's life in winters past. Jori loved these tales and asked many questions. Today, Astaga told stories of Shayana, who was on her mind since she had taken ill after the snow began falling.

"Did you know that Shayana invented drag sliding?" she asked the child.

"Shayana?" Jori's voice and face both reflected her amazement. "How did she do that?"

"When she was young, Shayana was an excellent Healer. One day she and other women were gathering herbs for medicines in the hills upstream. The hill was steep, and the drag that they piled with herbs got too heavy and started sliding down the soft grass. Stubborn Shayana did not just want to let it go, so she jumped on to stop the drag, but the slope was too slippery, and the drag kept sliding down the hill with her holding on to it!"

Jori laughed out loud.

"Shayana screamed all the way down to the river bank!" Astaga laughed. "I know you have only seen her as an angry old woman, but in those days Shayana was young and strong and smart, though already obstinate. She got up, dusted herself off, and pulled that drag back up the hill. Then she slid right down again, laughing all the way this time! She said it tickled her belly, and she kept at it until she learned how to steer the drag around trees and big rocks. When you ride your slide drag this winter, thank Shayana for your fun."

Jori became quiet. "She is very sick, is she not?"

"Yes, Jori, she is," Astaga looked directly at the girl.

"Will she pass over soon?" Jori asked with a steady gaze.

"Only The Mother knows, but if I had to guess, I would say that it is likely," the woman replied.

"Will Garnet still talk to her?" Jori asked. "She says she hears many spirits."

"I should not be surprised if Shayana keeps giving your

mother advice from the other side," Astaga smiled sardonically. "Some women in every generation hear the old ones, you know."

"What about Kelan?" Jori suddenly thought of her sister's experience with her own first kill.

"I do not know," Astaga said honestly. "If she can, it will surface."

"She understands the Bear Mother," Jori mused, "and when she saw my first kill, she seemed different afterwards. Perhaps she heard the buck's spirit leave this world."

"Yes, that is possible. She did seem to understand the Mother Bear both times they met," the woman nodded, "and you wonder if this means she will hear the ancestors?"

"Only The Mother knows," Jori said, smiling, "but if I had to guess, I would say that it is likely."

Jori was not surprised that afternoon when Barde came around to announce Shayana's passage. Astaga was seldom wrong about people, and Jori had earlier heard her mother talking to Healers about potions to help Shayana feel more comfortable. Jori remembered thinking at the time that they had not talked about healing Shayana, just easing her pain.

The next morning, everyone gathered in the Tribe house to bid the eldest goodbye. The Hechtas had bathed and dressed her body in her finest robes and wrapped her in warm furs. Women slipped small trinkets or tokens into her robes and furs, some giving little representations of The Mother they had carved to guide Shayana to the other side. Some placed special stones or feathers on her body in remembrance. Each woman and child was invited to approach and touch the old woman one last time. Some spoke out loud, others simply sat silently for a few moments before they went back outside.

Jori felt confused at all the sad feelings and went looking for

Daña, since her own mothers were too busy for questions right now.

Finding Daña near the big hearth, Jori asked, "Daña, why is everyone so sad that Shayana has died? They always complained about her."

Daña looked thoughtfully at the child. "Yes, sometimes Shayana annoyed us, but she was a woman of the Tribe. She was once a wonderful Healer and a good friend to many. We remember her lifetime, how she helped many women, and how great her heart was, not the infirmities of her old age," Daña's eyes were wet with tears. "When I was your age she took us out walking and fishing in the summer."

"So, you all loved her even though she annoyed you?" Jori wanted to know.

"Do you love Kelan even when you fight with her?" Daña asked.

"Not when I am angry, but after it passes. I never want anything bad to happen to her," Jori answered.

"So it was with Shayana," Daña explained, "and so it is with everyone in the Tribe. We do not always agree, but even when we argue, we are still family to one another."

Shayana's fur–wrapped body was laid gently onto a drag, and her knife and other tools were placed on top of her. Devin and Garnet, assisted by Herta, Nita, and Petrov, took her to a small cave that Shayana herself had chosen earlier. Inside, they laid her body out where the wall met the floor, and they carefully covered it with dirt and stones. They burned a special herb mixture that Nita concocted just for Shayana and offered a jug of wine to The Mother in gratitude for Shayana's presence in the Tribe's life.

Only the Queens and Hechtas knew all the words to the chants for the dead. The rest of the Tribeswomen followed them to the cave's entrance, where they sat and waited to escort the leaders back to the village.

Several days later, Garnet sat at the Hechtas' fire feeling disturbed by what she had heard. Barde told the Hechtas that Lia talked to other Tribeswomen about Jori and Kelan, saying that they should follow the paths of tradition, not the paths they themselves chose.

"Why would Lia suddenly try to sway opinions on this?" Garnet's confusion showed through her words. "She has never said those things to me."

"Barde asked Lia, who said that she honored Shayana's opinion since Shayana could no longer express it herself."

Garnet sighed, "I do not believe this!"

"Could it be that she is trying to take revenge on you for your lack of interest in her?" Herta asked.

"That is ridiculous!" Garnet snapped. "Why would she try to hurt the children?"

Shaking her head sadly, Herta said, "We cannot know what is in her mind, nor can we question her integrity. That will not convince anyone we are correct. We must address what she says, not why she says it."

"I agree," Marjika nodded, "and I do not think we should try to sway women before the Council. They will see our persuasion as worry about Lia's influence."

"Should we simply ignore this?" Devin felt angry and defensive, and her voice showed it.

"Yes, child," Astaga patted her knee. "We should simply act as if it is not important. If asked, just say that Lia is entitled to her opinion."

"Should we let Norahjen know what is happening when she returns?"

"I see no reason why we should," Astaga advised. "She

is trying to find peace as it is, and this would just anger her further."

"But Barde should continue to tell us what she hears," Garnet cautioned.

"She always does, dear," Herta told the Queen, "she always does."

"Marjika? Are you all right?" Garnet left her seat and knelt before the woman. "All the color has left your face. Are you in pain?"

Marjika nodded, clutching her abdomen. Her jaw was tight and she bit her lower lip. Devin and Herta carried her into the Temple. Garnet went for Anna and her medicines.

When she got to the Healers' house, though, she found Anna already delivering the other new one. She found only Lia was available, so the two of them returned swiftly to the Temple.

"Did your pains just begin?" Lia asked, kneeling over Marjika and brushing the hair gently from her eyes.

"I felt some discomfort this morning, but I thought it was just something I ate. Does Maya also give birth today?"

"Perhaps," Lia's tone was thoughtful. "She started having pains last night. Anna has been tending her, and she told me she thought the baby might come today, but Maya's last child took three nights to arrive, so we cannot be sure."

Marjika groaned at the thought, "Three nights!?!"

Lia chuckled, "This is your first child, Marjika. First children are sometimes in a hurry to arrive, and I do not think you will be that long."

Lia prepared a soothing tea for Marjika, who drank it gratefully. The Healer stayed the next several hours with the mother–to–be, making her walk as much as she was able. Lia said that walking eased the cramping and helped the child find its way out.

That evening, Garnet went to Maya's house to check on her

condition. She heard the newborn's first cries as she arrived and entered the house smiling.

Inside, she found Kelan helping Anna.

"Good fortune, Maya!" she kissed the woman's brow. The newborn squirmed in Maya's arms. Garnet looked at Anna, the unsaid question in her eyes. Anna smiled and nodded.

"It is male, and a big one, too! He looks quite healthy and strong."

Garnet let out the breath she had been holding and reached for the child. "May I?" she asked.

"Please," Maya handed him over to the Queen.

"Hello, my son," Garnet said softly to the child. His eyes sparkled at her. "You are heavy for a brand new one. That is good." The baby pursed his lips as if to suckle. "And you are hungry already!" Garnet was delighted the child looked so healthy.

"I will dream about you, my son," she promised him, "and when spring comes, I will give you a good name." Micah, said a voice in her head. Yes, she thought, that will do nicely, although it was really too soon to name the child. She must wait until the first buds showed on the fruit trees.

Garnet described Marjika's condition to Anna and Kelan, and she made Kelan promise to eat something before she came to the Temple to help. She assured the girl that the baby would wait for her.

Garnet took the happy news to Barde, who heard it with a grin. As Barde began her rounds of the village to announce the birth, Garnet returned to the Temple.

The baby girl did indeed wait for Kelan and for the sun to rise the next morning before she was born. Once the time came, the delivery was an easy one, attended by Lia, Kelan, and

Garnet. They cleaned baby and mother and changed the bedding before leaving to let them rest.

Walking back to the hearth, Kelan asked Garnet a question that surprised the woman.

"Mother, how do you learn their names?"

Garnet stopped walking. "Why?"

"When you were holding Maya's baby yesterday, I heard a name in my head," Kelan admitted.

"Yes, I did as well, but we cannot say it out loud! We do not speak a child's name until the naming day."

"Is that how you always get the names for new babies? You just hear a name?" Kelan asked again.

"Sometimes. Usually not so soon, though. Sometimes a name just comes to me like that; other times, I hold the baby and meditate a long time before I hear its name."

"Whose voice said the name?" Kelan wanted to know.

"I do not know, Kelan. Perhaps it was an ancestor of the child, or perhaps it was the inner voice of the child himself," Garnet told her.

"Does anyone else hear these things?" Kelan sounded nervous.

"A few hear the ancestors from time to time. I am not surprised that you have the gift," Garnet said, putting her arm gently around the girl. "Please tell me when you hear things so I can help you understand them, will you, dear?"

"All right, Mother."

"Remember, we must not speak the new babe's name yet, not until the spring," Garnet warned. "We never say a child's name out loud until it survives its first winter."

"I will not speak the name, then."

"Look. There goes Barde into the Tribe house," Garnet pointed. "She sings news of the second birth."

Barde entered the Tribe house and walked around the

hearth wall, singing, "A child is born into our Tribe. May she live to be healthy, happy, and wise."

"Another one? Is Marjika all right?" Devin grinned.

"Marjika is well and the child is vibrant," Barde said, stopping for a moment. "They enter the children's house this afternoon with Maya and her son."

"Thank you, good Barde," Devin bowed to the singer.

"I suppose my sister wants to stay with them," Jori sighed.

"Probably," Devin smiled. "She does love little children."

Finished with the subject, Jori changed it. "Devin, may we go sliding tomorrow if the sky is blue?"

Devin chuckled. "That is a good idea! I think I will come along, too."

The next morning, all the children except Kelan gathered at the Tribe house along with several adults. Some pulled drags behind them, and the group happily climbed the small hill between the village and the river. Women and girls plopped on drags and slid down the hill laughing. Some made it all the way down; some fell off their drags into the snow.

Devin's dogs followed the group, running up and down the hill and barking merrily. When Devin sat for her first ride, one of the dogs climbed onto her lap to ride down with her. But his wagging tail threw Devin off balance, and they both fell into the snow toward the bottom of the hill!

She jumped up laughing, then looped the drag's straps around the dog and ran up the hill, calling for him to follow. To everyone's astonishment, he happily ran up the hill, pulling the drag. Devin watched and wondered how she might use that skill some day. Perhaps, she thought, dogs could be trained to pull drags with supplies or people riding on them. Her faithful companions only learned a new skill if she taught it to them as a game, though, so she decided to think about this later and spend this time playing with the children and her four–pawed friends.

As Garnet left the children's house, she saw the big brown dog running into the village, pulling an empty drag tied to its back. She called the animal and it came to her, wagging its tail and shaking snow off. She was taking the drag's strap off him as the returning drag–sliders came into the village.

"Mother! Did you see the dog?" Jori yelled.

"They were sliding with us!" Ara shouted, gleeful.

"I saw him pulling the drag," Garnet laughed. "Poor pup," she said to the animal, scratching its ears. "They make you work wherever you go, do they not? If you keep working so hard, we will have to give you a name and make you a member of the tribe!"

"How are the babies?" Devin asked.

"Both are well," Garnet smiled, "and the mothers regain strength. Kelan is with them. I told her she could stay there tonight."

"By herself?" Jori was astounded at the major responsibility being given to her sister.

"She is very good, Jori. Having her with them is almost like having the Healer's apprentice there," Garnet's confidence mollified the girl.

"I told you!" Jori grinned at her parents. "I knew she would spend all her time with those babies."

"Have you even seen the new children yet?" Garnet thought she knew the answer.

"No."

"Well, come in and have a look," Garnet motioned for her daughter to enter.

Jori sighed and rolled her eyes at Devin, who grinned.

"Go on. Do as your mother says," Devin patted the girl's shoulder as she turned to follow Garnet.

The babies were adorable. Their tiny fingers clutched at the air, chubby cheeks glowed, and little black eyes sparkled. Jori took the boy into her arms awkwardly, and he smiled up at her.

"Oh, look!" she said excitedly. "He likes me!"

Kelan started to say something about the baby being too young to smile unless he had gas, but Garnet's upraised finger stopped her.

"Go dry yourself near the fire," Garnet told Jori, taking the baby. "The snow on you is melting and you are dripping. You will make him cold."

Kelan chewed her fingernails; sweat coated her skin. It was stiflingly warm in this building, and she was very nervous. Jori's leg jiggled against hers, broadcasting her own nervous energy.

Council Day had arrived at last, and every member of the Tribe gathered in the largest Tribe house. Garnet, Devin, all the Hechtas, Alecia, and two other Elders, Riah and Margaret, all sat together. The rest of the women sat around the big circle.

My, they are a noisy group, Garnet thought as she called the Tribe to order. She waited until she had everyone's attention before standing and walking over to the hearth, where she sprinkled an herb into the fire. A fragrant smoke rose and quickly scented the air with a sweetly pungent aroma. Finally, she spoke.

"I call upon The Mother and our mothers to join us today as we hold this Council. May we have the wisdom of our ancestors and the compassion of the Bear Mother. So be it."

"So be it," came the response.

She returned to her place and said, "All four who are at the age of choice have decided to remain with our Tribe. They will now announce the work they wish to do. Jena goes first, then Riala, then we will hear from Jori and Kelan. Jena, please tell the Elders and leaders your choice."

Jena stepped in front of the assembled leaders and Elders, and Garnet smiled at her encouragingly.

"I . . . wish to be a Healer," Jena said shyly.

"Why, Jena?" Marjika asked with a gentle voice.

"Why . . .?" Jena seemed confused by the question.

"Yes, child," Herta smiled at the girl. "Take your time and think on it. What makes you want to be a Healer?"

The girl thought a moment. "I have watched what the Healers do and it moves me. They are so calm, even when someone is badly injured, and I always want to help when someone is ill. It makes me feel . . . ummm . . . warm and needed."

Astaga nodded. "Good, Jena. Is there anything else you have considered doing?"

"No, Astaga," the girl replied.

"Does anyone wish to speak about Jena's choice of work?" Garnet looked at the Healers.

"I will be proud to have Jena as apprentice," Lia smiled at the girl.

"I, too, find her acceptable," Anna added, "so long as she does well at her initial training."

"Does anyone object to this girl's choice?" Garnet asked.

She let the silence stretch out.

"Good. Jena, report to the Healers on the new moon to begin your training," Garnet hugged the beaming girl. "Serve the Tribe well, my daughter."

"I will." Jena walked back around the hearth to where her mother sat.

Garnet, smiling now, said, "Riala, please approach."

Riala came around the hearth and stood before the leaders and Elders, shaking.

"Fear us not, child," Alecia said kindly. "Your choice is sacred. There must be a very strong and compelling reason for the Tribe to deny you."

Garnet looked at Devin, who smiled warmly.

"What is your choice, Riala?" she said, touching the girl comfortingly.

"I love to cook," Riala said with a trembling voice, "and I have helped the Fire Tenders many times. I would like to apprentice myself to the Cooks."

"Why, Riala?" Garnet repeated the question.

Riala stood silently a moment before she found the words. "When I feed people, I feel like I am giving life to them and so to the Tribe."

"Well said!" Nita smiled.

"Wren?" Garnet asked the Cook. "How do you feel about Riala's choice?"

"She has a good head and sure hands," Wren told them. "I am glad she chooses to work among us."

"Any objections?" Garnet asked the Tribe. Everyone smiled and stayed silent.

"Good. Riala, report to Wren on the new moon," Garnet released the girl with a nod.

"I have tea ready," Wren told the women. "Let us have a sip and congratulate these girls before we go to the rest of our work."

She passed out tea to the women. When she served the two Queens, Devin leaned over and whispered, "Good idea, my friend."

Wren poured and said quietly, "The tea will calm everyone."

Garnet grinned. Wren had made tea with soothing herbs and she hoped it would help.

When the women finished drinking tea and all had congratulated Riala and Jena, Garnet called them back together.

"I feel that we must consider Jori and Kelan together since their futures are intertwined. Daughters, please come and speak to the Tribe."

The girls rose and approached the panel, clutching hands. They let go of one another, and Jori took a deep breath and spoke first.

"Elders, leaders, and women of the Tribe," she began, "you have all known us since birth. You know that the Hearth Queen and the Hunt Queen have raised the two of us as sisters. Both are my mothers. As Kelan and I have grown up, we have each discovered the things that bring us joy. I am happiest when I am out hunting, or sitting in a tall tree's branches with Swain, or working on a project with Daña. Devin's calling is also my own. I cherish my duty to the Tribe. I will serve you well, but I cannot be your Hearth Queen. I choose to be Hunt Queen."

The crowd murmured many reactions, some of admiration at the girl's courage, some unhappy to hear the plain truth stated so boldly. Garnet raised her hand and silenced them all.

"Our chance to speak and question will come in due time," Garnet said authoritatively, "but first, let us hear from both girls. Kelan?"

Kelan stood and nodded respectfully to each leader and Elder. She looked at each woman as she spoke.

"My mothers, my leaders, my sisters, I love you all, and like Jori, you have watched me from birth. You have seen my love for babies, my abilities as a Healer, and my mother can tell you of my beginnings with 'majik' . I wish to prepare myself to serve the Tribe as Hearth Queen on some far–away day. I am no good at hunting or building. I do not care to learn strangers' ways or trade with them as my sister does. I think that I could learn those things if I had to, but I do not find joy in them. I have been taught since I was old enough to hear that the most sacred thing of all is a woman's choice. I ask you today to honor my choice and the choice of my sister," Kelan finished and looked at Garnet.

"You know the tradition, child," Alecia's strident tone challenged them both. "For generations of generations, the daughter of the Hearth Queen has become the Hearth Queen."

"We do know, Elder," Kelan answered, "but we are both daughters of the Hearth Queen and we are both daughters of the Hunt Queen as well," she said, looking warmly at her mothers.

"Ridiculous!" Alecia snapped. "Two mothers??!! You were born to only one woman!"

"But, Elder," Jori said, "we were raised by both."

Garnet felt her jaw tighten. She could not answer for the girls, though she dearly wished she could. But if they were to win the support of the Tribe as its future leaders, the women must respect them for expressing their own views.

"What does that matter?" Alecia snapped at them.

"When a child's mother dies and another woman takes her in and cares for her, that woman is considered her mother, is she not?" Herta interrupted.

"Yes, but these girls' mothers live!" Alecia raised her voice now.

"I am just saying that there are times when we consider a woman who did not give birth to a child as the child's mother." Herta looked around the room. "Does anyone in this room question the love of Devin and Garnet for both children?"

There was an uncomfortable silence.

"I know," said Lia, sounding reasonable, "that we must consider the girls' wishes, and it is obvious which tasks each enjoys.

But as Kelan said herself, she CAN learn the tasks required of her as Hunt Queen, she simply does not WISH to."

"I think there is a voice that speaks louder than tradition. The Great Bear Mother Herself has chosen Kelan for Hearth Queen!" Marjika interjected hotly. "By allowing only Kelan to go near Her cub and by allowing Kelan to rescue little Ara, She showed that She trusts Kelan with the Tribe's children."

"I agree with Marjika," Astaga's voice was calmer but still firm. "Many times over generations, the Great Bear Mother has made Her wishes known."

"Jori has made kills," Tem added, "and not just rabbits! She is the youngest Tribe member ever to kill an antlered animal, and this summer, she got two of them. When the Bear spared Ara, Jori wisely offered Her the reindeer that she had just killed. I will gladly follow Jori."

"As will I," Daña looked the girl in the eye and added, "in many years, when she is older."

"But it is against tradition!" Alecia insisted.

"There have been times . . ." Astaga started to say.

"Do not tell one of your stories, Astaga!" Alecia shouted.

"Your mind is closed and locked tight!" Astaga shouted back. "If you will not see the truth when it is right in front of you, you should not be in a position to decide these children's fate!"

Everyone spoke or shouted at once. Garnet stood tall and raised her hands.

"ENOUGH!" she bellowed, and a sudden, resounding silence fell over the room. "This is a Tribal Council meeting, not one of those wrestling matches the men hold! We must act with respect and care for one another so that we may each have a say in this. No one will be silenced, and no one," with a pointed look to Alecia, "will be interrupted. In this Tribe, every woman gets her say, even if we talk for an entire moon cycle! After every woman who wishes has spoken, we will retire to our homes and consider everything that we have heard. We will meet again tomorrow to see if we have found agreement.

"I will take the Queen's prerogative and speak first. I love both of these girls deeply, and I have watched them both all their lives. I hope you agree that, more than anyone else, I know what is required of the Hearth Queen. I tell you this: From everything I have witnessed and from everything that all of you have told me about these girls, Kelan is the clear choice to follow me. I love Jori dearly. She is my own blood, and I have no doubt that she can learn the necessary skills," Garnet took a deep breath and looked kindly at her daughter, "but she does not have the 'majik' and she would be miserable trying to be Hearth Queen. An unhappy woman is good at nothing. I ask you to allow these girls their sacred choices." She sat down.

Devin stood to say, "I, too, love both girls deeply, and I hope you agree that I know what is required of the Hunt Queen. I tell you, Jori will make the strongest, most capable Hunt Queen in anyone's memory. While Kelan is very talented, she hates everything she would have to do as my apprentice. The Tribe flourishes when all are happy and content. Forcing the girls into positions they hate is not a good decision for them, nor is it good for any of us."

Norahjen stood. "I agree with the Queens. The Hechtas have also watched both girls since birth. We believe that both girls are remarkable and talented. Jori is a skilled Hunter and a capable builder already, and Kelan has the very essence of 'majik' in her soul. I urge you to accept the girls' choices. To do otherwise dishonors The Mother."

Each Hechta stood in her turn and each said she honored the girls' choices. When the Elders' turns came, Riah expressed reservations about breaking tradition, and Margaret said that she would honor the girls' choices if the rest of the Tribe consented. Alecia, as expected, talked at great length about tradition and how the Tribe would meet a terrible fate if they altered something this basic to their ways. By the time the leaders, Hechtas, and Elders had all spoken, the sun was setting and stomachs growled for dinner. Wren called a halt to the discussion long enough to feed everyone, and then they returned to Council.

Every woman in the Tribe had the opportunity to speak. Many supported the girls, but some did not. Lia was directly hostile to the idea and said so strongly. Garnet thought Lia was persuasive and feared that she had influenced some women to her position. Some said that they would not follow Kelan as Hearth Queen or Jori as Hunt Queen. Some said they did not know the right path.

It was late into the night by the time each woman had either spoken or passed. Garnet encouraged them to stay in silence for the rest of the night and think about all they had heard. She suggested they not discuss the issues with anyone else so that each woman could better hear her own inner voice and find the truth she most deeply believed.

Neither girl slept well that night. Kelan lay in her sleeping fur but tossed and turned all night long. When she did drop off to sleep, nightmares woke her often. She was an elk walking through the trees. She felt the ground under her hooves and the leaves brushing against her fur as she dodged branches. She panicked, made a quick turn to the right, and felt something burning in her left flank with a sudden, intense pain. She tripped and fell, rolling onto her side and struggling to stand. She felt someone towering over her, and when she looked up, the face looking down at her was her very own!

Jori sat on the ledge at the hearth fire in the Tribe house and stared into the flames for most of the night. She saw a very real possibility that the Tribe might require her to become Hearth Queen. It just was not fair! Every other woman had a choice!

Different things that different women had said throughout

the Council went round and round in her mind. Herta the Rememberer said there was one time when the Hearth Queen's daughter died while still young, and the daughter of the Hunt Queen was named Hearth Queen in her place.

Lia's answer to the story echoed in Jori's mind, "I will not follow Kelan while the daughter of the Hearth Queen lives." Many other women agreed. "While the daughter lives . . ." echoed over and over in Jori's mind. "While the daughter lives . . ."

I know, Jori thought. I can leave the Tribe and live in the wild by myself! If I leave, at least Kelan can follow her path and be happy. I can hunt and I know how to make fire. I can find herbs and kartof. She thought of the caves near the Bear's lair. Bears hibernated all through the winter, so she thought she might be safe as long as she did not enter the Bear's own cave.

Jori stood resolutely, her decision made. It was for the good of the Tribe. Someone else could be Hunt Queen, but it was important that Kelan become Hearth Queen.

She walked through the snow to Devin's house, hearing not a sound in the village. She crept to the door and peered inside to see no one home. She gathered her bow and quiver, a knife of Devin's, some food, and extra furs. She tucked it all into a pack and slung the pack over her shoulder.

Jori stopped at the big trench to relieve herself quickly before her long, cold walk. The sky was turning light where the sun rose, and she wanted to be long gone before others woke up. As she adjusted her clothing, she heard someone approach and relaxed when she saw Ara.

"What are you doing up so early?" Jori whispered.

"I had to go," Ara smiled at her friend, then saw the pack on Jori's back. "Where are you going?"

"Do not tell," Jori said. "I have decided to leave the Tribe and live alone."

"What?" Ara was stunned.

"Shhh! Do not wake everyone," Jori quieted her friend. "Remember when Herta told us about the daughter of the Hearth Queen who died?"

"Yes, but . . ." Ara began.

"No, just listen," Jori pleaded. Ara nodded, and she continued, "Alecia and Lia have convinced some of the women that Kelan and I should not have our choices, but if I am gone, perhaps they will let Kelan become Hearth Queen. Then at least one of us will be happy."

"Where will you go?" Ara feared for her friend. "How will you live?"

"I go to the caves near where we saw the Bears. I can build fires and hunt. I will be fine," Jori told her, trying to reassure her friend in spite of her own fears. "Maybe when you get older you can come and visit me there."

"The Bears will attack you!" Ara blurted.

"No. They sleep all winter long. I will go to the sea in the spring before they awaken," Jori touched her friend's face. "Go back to your house, and please, tell no one that you saw me! Kelan must be Hearth Queen, and I am doing what I must for the Tribe." She ran into the darkness.

Later that morning the entire Tribe came to Council again in the big house, but no one could find Jori.

"Do you know where she is?" Garnet asked Kelan.

"I have not seen her since last night," Kelan replied.

"The night–time Fire Keeper said she sat here staring at the flames most of the night, then she left," Wren reported.

"I will look for her," Tem left the house.

But Jori was no where to be found anywhere in the village.

By afternoon, Jori found the cave she sought, the one where they first saw the Bear and Her cub in the tree. Vines shielded the entrance, but she found her way in. Jori searched the small cave thoroughly and found no recent trace of animals.

Walking around the plateau to get a feel for the terrain of her new home, she scooped up snow to melt for water and took it back into the cave. She built a small fire just outside the entrance and made some tea, then ate bread and dried fish she had brought. She decided to hunt tomorrow.

She was so tired! She had not slept at all last night, and today she had walked far. She was fast asleep before her head even reached the furs.

Back at the village the Cooks prepared a meal, but few had the heart to eat as everyone worried about Jori. They talked all day and finally reached agreement about the girls' choices. It was one of the most difficult Councils anyone living could remember, but finally, they all agreed.

Late in the afternoon Garnet sat near the hearth drinking tea that Lia brought her.

"I am sorry, Garnet," Lia told the Queen. "I was so angry with you that I could not see my nose at the front of my face. I did not wish to hurt the girls, only to oppose you."

Garnet patted the woman's hand. "You meant no harm, Lia."

"I think I will stay in the Temple for a time. I need some dark time, to look into myself and find the light again," Lia told the Queen.

Devin stood over little Ara, looking serious. She had noticed both sadness and fear on Ara's face through the day, and she wondered if the child knew something she was not telling. She tried to convince the girl to reveal any secrets she might have about Jori.

"I know you promised Jori you would not tell," Devin was

adamant. "but it is winter, and she might die of the cold. You MUST tell me what you know!"

Ara looked at Daña, who nodded. Then she spoke.

"Jori talked about what Herta said, about the time the daughter of the Hearth Queen died and the daughter of the Hunt Queen replaced her as Hearth Queen. She said that if she went away at least Kelan could be happy."

"Oh, Mother of us all!" Devin spat. "That child and her ideas!"

"Did she say where she was going, Ara?" Tem asked the frightened child.

"To the caves where we saw the Bear," Ara confessed. "She said since the Bears sleep in the winter, she would be in no danger from them."

"It is dangerous to climb those rocky hills in the snow." Daña looked at Devin.

"I will ask Swain to come with me and track her," Devin turned to go.

Tem and Daña both stood. "We go, too, my friend," Daña said.

They all strode to the Tribe house and told Garnet and other waiting women what they had learned. Garnet wanted to go, too, but Devin would not hear of it.

"One of us must stay here, darling. The Tribe cannot risk us both." She kissed Garnet and held her for a moment before leaving.

Jori awoke in full darkness to the sound of a familiar voice.

"Here she is!" yelled Tem over her shoulder. The awakening child was suddenly pulled from her sleeping furs and hugged hard.

"You gave us a scare, young Hunter!" Tem told the child,

ignoring her protests and carrying her outside. Tem planted the girl's feet firmly on the snowy ground.

Jori was confused and barely awake until her bare feet touched cold snow, which made her yelp in shock. She looked across the plateau and saw torches bobbing up the hill. Devin ran toward her, followed by Swain and the rest of the Hunters.

"I should make you walk home without your boots!" Devin raged at the child, teary eyed. She picked Jori up off the ground and hugged her tight. "You little scamp! You could have died out here!"

"But then Kelan could be Hearth Queen," Jori said quietly. Devin looked into the serene little face. What an amazing woman this child was becoming!

"She will anyway," she told the girl, "and you will be Hunt Queen if you do not die from your own recklessness before you grow up!"

"What . . .?" Jori was confused. "They said that we could not change!"

"The Hunters told the Tribe this morning that they would follow no one except you or me. They said that if the Tribe wanted to eat, they must accept your choice," Devin explained.

"Then the others said they supported you, too," Swain told her, grinning, "and the Scout spoke up as well."

"Go get your things, young hothead," Tem tousled the girl's tangled hair. "We have a Tribe to feed and house, and we cannot stand on this mountain all day talking about it!"

"We have already talked for two days!" Swain laughed. "That is more talking than I have heard in many seasons!"

Jori gathered her things and the entire party escorted her to the village. By the time they approached home the sun was peeking across the horizon. As they crossed the flats, women and children ran to greet them. Garnet flew to the child and picked her up, covering her face and neck with kisses.

"Dear Jori, I was worried sick for you!"

"I am sorry to scare you, Mother. I am all right," Jori squirmed to get out of the tight grasp. When she finally got back on her feet, she saw Kelan standing quietly by.

"You did this for me?" Kelan asked.

"You are my sister," Jori said simply and hugged her.

"We may each have our own choice," Kelan said with tears in her eyes. "Are you sure this is your desire?"

"I am sure. You will be Hearth Queen, and it is my destiny to protect and serve you and the Tribe as Hunt Queen all of my days."

Winter
1984 C.E.

Through the winter we sat in the cabin in front of her fireplace, our hands busy with projects. While we whittled, wove baskets, or braided leather strips, she spoke.

I listened to stories from untold generations of our people, how we lived, changed, and almost all died out. I learned about the Tribe and its progress through centuries. I learned about the spring when we built a village and stopped being nomads.

Before I left, she lifted a worn pouch of seeds from around her wrinkled neck and handed it to me. She said it held seeds from that first season, and she instructed me to guard them and pass them along to the next Rememberer. This first book is about that time.

I learned about the summer we traded for our first wagon, about the fall we first saw horses, about the winter our Tribe and another joined forces in defense. I am writing these stories and others now.

In the end, I came to know that the Tribe exists still. I came to believe that no matter how far we have traveled from that first village along the Olt, we can always go home because our homes are in the hearts of one another.

I am home whenever I go where women gather. I am home when I sit at the festival night stage. I am home in a church basement where women sit on cold metal folding chairs and talk about resisting oppression, fighting for justice. I am home in the Temple Room at the RCGI Motherhouse, being taught by Jade or Bellezza or Kim.

I am home whenever I look into the eyes of another woman and see my own heart.

About the Author

Kip Parker is a Dianic witch and a member of the Re–Formed Congregation of the Goddess, International. Kip is currently pursuing a Mistress of Wicca degree in RCG's famed Women's Thealogical Institute (www.rcgi.org). She lives in the hinterlands of Middle America, surrounded by her eclectic lesbian family. At midlife she has found the love of her life and the courage to tell the stories that have lived within her for untold millennia. She maintains three things from her youth: Phred, her old black guitar; her quick wits; and her smart mouth. She believes strongly three things: in the love of women; in unsettling anyone who is absolutely sure of anything; and in laughing in church. She thinks that the worst thing any writer (or politician) can do is to take themselves too seriously. Her advice to young women: Act up! Laugh a lot! And don't be afraid to make your mistakes.

Contact the Author

Contact Kip through the publisher (information below). Kip encourages all interested readers to check out the website of the Re–formed Congregation of the Goddess, International at www.rcgi.org. Kip is available for workshops, signings and discussions. *Creatrix Books LLC* will forward all correspondence directly to Kip.

About Creatrix Vision Spun Fiction LLC

The Planting Rite is the first invaluable addition to the *Creatrix Vision Spun Fiction LLC* imprint. The second addition, *She Who Walks the Labyrinth* by Kassandra G. Sojourner, is due out fall 2006. For further information about either of these books, please contact us through *Creatrix Books LLC*, information below. *Creatrix Vision Spun Fiction* is a Wisconsin Limited Liability company and a *Creatrix Books LLC* company.

About Creatrix Books LLC

Creatrix Books LLC is woman owned and operated and was founded to give a voice to Goddess and her children via the written word.

Creatrix Books LLC
PO Box 366
Cottage Grove, WI 53527
www.creatrixbooks.com